GIN AND BEAR IT

What Reviewers Say
About Joy Argento's Work

Exes and O's

"I really appreciated the new take on a burned lover in Ali. Instead of pushing love away forever, she decides to actively seek out what has gone wrong in order to do better in her future. I also enjoyed how the story focuses on what a healthy relationship should be and how to get to that. It was refreshing. ...If you're in the mood for a gentle second-chance romance that has just enough angst, great character development, and will have you dying for a donut, run for this book!"—*Lesbian Review*

Before Now

"*Before Now* by Joy Argento is a mixture of modern day romance and historical fiction. ...There was some welcome humour and a bit of angst. An interesting story well told."—*Kitty Kat's Book Review Blog*

Emily's Art and Soul

"...the leads are well rounded and credible. As a 'friends to lovers' romance the author skillfully transforms their budding friendship to an increasing intimacy. Mindy, Emily's Down syndrome sister, is a great secondary character, very realistic in her traits and interactions with other people. Her fresh outlook on life and her 'best friend' declarations help to keep the upbeat tone."—*LezReviewBooks*

"This was such a sweet book. Great story that would be perfect as a holiday read. The plot was fun and the pace really good. The protagonists were enjoyable and Emily's character was well fleshed out. …This is the first book I've read by Joy Argento and it won't be the last. I'm looking forward to what comes next."
—*Rainbow Literary Society*

Visit us at www.boldstrokesbooks.com

By the Author

Emily's Art and Soul

Before Now

Carrie and Hope

No Regrets

Exes and O's

Missed Conception

Gin and Bear It

GIN AND BEAR IT

by
Joy Argento

2023

GIN AND BEAR IT

ISBN 13: 978-1-63679-351-1

THIS TRADE PAPERBACK ORIGINAL IS PUBLISHED BY
BOLD STROKES BOOKS, INC.
P.O. BOX 249
VALLEY FALLS, NY 12185

FIRST EDITION: APRIL 2023

CREDITS
EDITOR: CINDY CRESAP
PRODUCTION DESIGN: SUSAN RAMUNDO
COVER DESIGN BY TAMMY SEIDICK AND JOY ARGENTO

Acknowledgments

I would like to thank the readers who have taken the time to read my books and leave reviews. Your support has kept my fingers moving across the keyboard spitting out stories that would have made my brain explode if they didn't come out. Thanks for keeping my head intact.

Thank you to my editor, Cindy Cresap. Your words of encouragement mean the world to me.

Special thanks to Olessia Butenko and Tobie Hewitt for finding all the mistakes that I miss. I am so grateful for you.

Thank you to my support system, without whom I would probably curl up in a ball and suck my thumb.

Kate Klansky
Susan Carmen-Duffy
Karin Cole
Georgia Beers
Barbara DiFiore
And my kids, Jamie, Jess, and Tony

Chapter One

I'd get rid of Paula before I'd rehome Bear," Rachel said.
"But she's allergic to cats. If I don't rehome him, she said she won't come over anymore. And we can't go to her house because her mother is living with her, and she doesn't approve of Paula being gay." Kelly James sipped her sloe gin fizz, letting the fruity flavor envelop her mouth. She felt guilty enough about Bear without Rachel making her feel worse.

She shifted her weight on the tall barstool. She would have been more comfortable at a table with the shorter chairs, but Rachel liked sitting at the bar. Who was she fooling? She had her reasons for sitting at the bar too.

"Did she tell you she was allergic before?"

Kelly thought about it for a moment. No, she hadn't. But Kelly didn't have a cat when she and Paula met eight months ago. So there was no reason for her to mention it. Getting Bear while Paula was out of town on business wasn't something Kelly had planned on, but when her friend Marley called and told her about the stray looking for a new home two weeks ago, Kelly thought she could provide a good one for him. She had no idea it would cause such a problem for her girlfriend.

"Well?" Rachel asked. Patience had never been her strong suit. She was a *tell it like it is* kind of person. Kelly usually loved that about her. Not so much at the moment.

"No. But she didn't have a reason to before. I've only had Bear for a couple of weeks. I've had her for eight months."

"I thought it was a rule that all lesbians had to like cats," Rachel said.

"I said she was allergic, not that she didn't like him. Besides, you aren't crazy about them."

"I'm bi," Rachel said. "We don't have a strict set of rules like your people do."

Kelly tilted her head "My people?"

"You know. Lesbians. Kelly, you're thirty-four years old, for God's sake. You should be able to keep your cat if you want to."

Kelly shook her head. "That's exactly the point. I'm thirty-four years old. This is my last chance at love. I'm not willing to give it up."

"What are you talking about? You make it sound like you're over the hill. I'm three years older than you."

Kelly drained the remainder of her drink and motioned the female bartender over. The very hot female bartender, with her dark blond hair that hung down a few inches above her shoulders and dimples that could kill you if you looked at them long enough. Her black button-down shirt was neatly pressed, and she had the sleeves rolled up several turns, almost to her shoulders, showing off very toned arms. She wore very little makeup, mostly just a bit of eye liner and maybe mascara. It was hard to tell; her lashes were so thick they probably didn't need any help.

Kelly and Rachel always sat at the bar so she would be the one serving them, despite the barstool's lack of comfort for Kelly. Rachel, being a few inches taller, never seemed to have a problem with them. They'd checked out several of the bars in the area in the past couple of years, but the Queen of Hearts was their favorite. They didn't play loud, obnoxious music, so you could actually have a conversation, and the lighting was adequate enough that you could read the menu if you wanted to order snacks. The hot bartender was certainly an added bonus. They had yet to find out her name.

The place had been around for at least several decades and had changed hands a few times. Rachel said it was twice. Kelly was sure it was three. The newest owner had replaced the old well-worn bar top with a new, fine grain wooden top—oak, Kelly guessed, and had taken the obnoxiously large mirror out from behind the bar. Kelly was grateful. She hated when she caught her own reflection in it. She was convinced that she never looked good, especially when she was sitting next to Rachel or worse yet when Hot Bartender was near her.

Kelly turned her attention back to her friend. "It doesn't matter how old *you* are. You have a husband. And besides, you're beautiful." Mark, Rachel's husband, was equally as good-looking. They were the kind of couple that turned heads when they walked into a room. Mark didn't seem to mind that Rachel drooled over beautiful women. He knew she was bi way before they got married.

"Refill?" Hot Bartender asked Kelly.

She nodded, barely glancing at her. Kelly knew that if she gave the woman her full attention, she'd end up staring. She was that off the charts hot.

"Me too, please," Rachel said.

The bartender took their empty glasses and set about making them fresh drinks.

"Do you know how crazy you are?" Rachel asked Kelly.

"Why, because I want another drink?"

"No. Because you are always putting yourself down."

"How am I putting myself down?"

"You are so darn cute it's ridiculous. But you think you can't do better than Paula because you don't think you're good enough."

"I have at least fifteen extra pounds on me, my nose isn't straight, my ears stick out, and I'm not outgoing. With all these flaws I'm lucky to have Paula."

"That's why I said you're crazy. And I can follow that up by saying you're full of crap. I don't know what you see when you look in the mirror, but no one else sees what you do."

Ms. Hot returned with their new drinks.

Kelly slid two bills across the bar to her. "Keep the change," she said without making eye contact.

"Did you see that?" Rachel asked.

"See what?"

"She smiled at you. Super-hot Bartender smiled at you."

"Of course, she did. I just gave her a decent tip."

"You should get her phone number." Rachel took a sip from her glass. "And she makes the best damn drinks. What more could you ask for?"

"She may be hot, but she doesn't have the best reputation around here. I hear she's more into one-night stands than relationships."

"Nothing wrong with that. I would have a one-night stand with her if Mark wouldn't insist on joining us."

"You're a liar. You would never do that. I know you and I know how much you love him. Why can't you understand that I want the same thing? Paula and I are heading in that direction."

"Did she say that? Has she talked about marriage—or even moving in together?"

Kelly pulled the lemon slice off the rim of her glass and flicked her tongue against it. It made her mouth pucker, but she knew her drink would taste even sweeter in contrast. "No. But she can't think about that right now."

"Her mother lives with her," both Kelly and Rachel said in unison.

"Shut up," Kelly said. "The timing just isn't right."

Rachel just didn't understand. She and Mark had been together for ten years and married for six. She couldn't possibly know how hard it was to find someone at this age. And meeting a single gay woman was especially hard when you didn't go out much and worked at a solitary job as a dog walker.

"So, you're really going to do it? You're going to give Bear up?"

"What choice do I have?"

"You don't really want me to answer that, do you?"

Kelly shook her head. No, she knew exactly what Rachel would say. But it was either give up Bear or give up Paula, probably forever. "I'm not bringing him to a shelter. I want to find him a good home where I can visit him."

"I guess that's better than abandoning him altogether." Rachel pushed a lock of red hair behind her ear. Kelly envied that hair. Every piece stayed in place. And that new short bob looked so good on her. Kelly couldn't seem to control her hair no matter what length or style she wore.

"Thanks for making me feel worse about this." Kelly took a large swig of her drink.

Rachel rubbed Kelly's back. "I'm sorry. I know this isn't easy on you. I just wish there was another way. I would take him, but Jack would probably terrorize him to death. You know that old dog doesn't like cats."

"I know. I'll think of something. Paula said she can't come over until he's gone."

"She actually said *that*? Until he's gone?"

Kelly wished she hadn't said anything. She knew admitting that, yes indeed, that was exactly how Paula had said it, would make Paula seem heartless. But Kelly was all about honesty and there wasn't a way to answer without Paula looking bad. So she ignored the question.

"She did. No need to answer. How do you want to do this? Find Bear a new home? I'll help you."

"Who's Bear?" Hot Bartender was back.

"He's my cat," Kelly said, staring into her drink, watching the ice move as she swirled the glass.

"Why do you have to find him a new home?"

Kelly was embarrassed to answer. Not that she was choosing her girlfriend over a pet she'd only had a couple of weeks, but because she had taken responsibility for an animal that she couldn't keep.

"Her girlfriend is allergic," Rachel answered for her.

"That's too bad. I might be interested. Can you tell me about him?"

Kelly raised her eyes to the bartender's. They were deep green, the color of an emerald with what could only be described as a *sparkle,* the kind you only read about in books. "Seriously?" She held her gaze and found a kindness there she hadn't expected. Her breath caught in her throat.

"Absolutely. I live above the bar here. It's not a huge apartment, but there's a big bedroom and a half bathroom, so there's plenty of room for a litter box and room for him to roam. I'm home a lot and usually go upstairs on my breaks, so he wouldn't be alone much."

I'll bet you aren't alone much, Kelly thought. Not with those dimples and toned arms and those... She shook the thoughts away.

"She needs him to go somewhere she can visit him. Even though she's only had him a little while, she's attached," Rachel said.

"I can understand that. I had my cat for almost eighteen years. I lost him three months ago. It's been lonely without him. And it would be no problem for you to visit." She put her hand out. "I'm Logan Spencer by the way."

Kelly briefly shook the hand that was offered to her. But she didn't respond. She couldn't seem to speak. Those eyes. Those dimples. That face.

"That's Kelly James," Rachel said. "I'm Rachel Pruitt."

Logan shook her hand as well. "I didn't mean to put you on the spot, Kelly. I can tell this is really hard for you." She put her hands up and started to back away.

"Wait," Kelly said. "It is hard. But I don't want to give him to just anyone. How did you lose your cat?"

Logan took a step closer. "Well, at eighteen he really was an old man. He developed an upper respiratory infection he just couldn't fight off." Tears filled her eyes. Her incredible eyes. She wiped them as they spilled over her thick bottom lashes and down her cheeks. She didn't seem the least bit embarrassed to show emotion in front of strangers.

Kelly was touched. Logan must have really cared about her cat. Maybe she could care about Bear just as much. "The vet guessed Bear to be about two. We don't know for sure because he was an unclaimed stray. I made sure he had all his shots and he's been dewormed and of course neutered. He's been an indoor cat since I got him, and he doesn't seem to mind. He's great at using the litter box." She pulled her phone out of the back pocket of her jeans, turned it so Logan could see, and scrolled through the pictures.

"He's beautiful," Logan said. "And he looks like a sweetheart."

Kelly glanced at the phone. The last picture was a selfie she took of Bear curled up with her on the couch. Damn it. She didn't mean to scroll that far. Bear looked great in all the photos. Kelly was never crazy about the way she looked. "You can come over and meet him if you want. You know, to see if it would be a good match."

Logan's face lit up. Kelly didn't think that face could have gotten any more beautiful, but she was wrong. That smile took it to a whole new level. She glanced at Rachel. If she had been a cartoon her tongue would be hanging out of her mouth and her eyes bulging out of her head. She was staring at Logan that intently.

"I would love that." A customer on the other end of the bar waved Logan over. "Be back in a few." She put her hand on the bar in front of Kelly. "Don't leave."

Kelly stared down at the hand in front of her. She loved Paula. So why did she have such a strong desire to place her hand on top of Logan's and feel the warmth and softness of it?

"That woman should be a model," Rachel said, staring after her. "Not that too thin, ultra fem model, but the one that has a natural beauty that shines through so strong it can give you a sunburn."

"Put your eyes back in your head. Do I have to remind you that you're married?" Kelly said.

"I know. I know. I can look. I'm not touching. Tell me you don't think she's beautiful?"

"She's okay."

Rachel bumped her shoulder, spilling a few drops of the drink Kelly had just picked up. She lifted the glass higher, trying to avoid spilling it on her shirt. She was successful for the most part. "Hey."

"Come on. She's more than okay and you know it. You aren't so in love with *Paula* that you're blind to a beautiful woman."

Kelly didn't like the way Rachel said Paula's name. She made no secret of the fact that she didn't like her. Kelly didn't know why. She'd only met her once at Kelly's apartment. She was the only one of Kelly's friends who had met Paula, even though they'd been dating for months. Paula liked it to be just the two of them when they were together. She didn't even like to go out in public together, preferring to keep Kelly all to herself, she said. Kelly thought it was sweet—most of the time. Although if she was being honest with herself, she often hated that they never went out or did things—anything—except share an occasional meal, watch a movie, or have sex. Those were all great, but it would have been nice to go for a walk, eat in a restaurant, or anything else that would get them out of Kelly's apartment.

"You don't like older women?" Rachel asked.

"How do you know how old she is?"

"I know things." Rachel sipped her drink. "I asked Joe." Joe was the bartender on Logan's days off. They both worked on Friday and Saturday night.

"You asked her age, but you never bothered to ask her name?" Kelly shook her head.

"I just asked about the hottie behind the bar. He didn't offer her name and I didn't even think to ask."

"Why did you ask her age?"

"Because I couldn't quite pinpoint it. She has old soul eyes—like she's seen a lot. But there isn't a single wrinkle on that beautiful mug."

"There isn't, is there? I have this one forming on my forehead." Kelly raised her eyebrows.

"Everyone gets a wrinkle there when they do that," Rachel said.

"Are you going to tell me how old she is or just keep talking about it?"

Rachel fished the cherry out of her drink and popped it in her mouth before answering. "I thought you didn't care."

"I don't. Just curious."

"She's…" Rachel let the word trail off as Logan made her way back toward them.

"Sorry about that," Logan said. "You were saying I can come over and meet Bear. I would love to do that."

"Are you working tomorrow evening?" Kelly asked, even though she knew the answer. Wednesdays and Sundays were Joe's shifts. Logan wouldn't be working.

"As a matter of fact, I'm not. I'm supposed to help my mom with a few things, but I can be done by five or six. If that works for you. I don't want to interrupt your dinnertime or your time with your girlfriend."

"Her girlfriend won't come over as long as Bear lives there," Rachel volunteered.

Kelly gave her a sideways glance that she hoped would convey the message to shut up.

Logan's eyes shifted from Rachel to Kelly. "I don't want to cause any trouble."

Kelly cleared her throat. "It's no trouble. I don't usually eat any kind of formal dinner. I just grab whatever." She let a beat or two pass in silence before adding, "I know I should probably plan my meals better. I mean I'm trying to lose weight, and if I plan—"

"You should eat whenever and whatever you want. Life's too short to worry about stuff like that," Logan said.

Kelly was surprised at her response. She looked like she took good care of herself, probably only ate health food, and definitely worked out—a lot. "Um…anyway, five or six works."

"Can I have your phone again?" Logan asked.

Kelly hesitated, confused.

Rachel discreetly elbowed her. "It's in your back pocket."

"I know." She didn't need Rachel making her look like a fool—she was capable of doing that all on her own. She handed her phone to Logan.

Logan tapped on it and turned it back toward Kelly. Kelly watched as it registered her face and unlocked. She was still confused.

Logan typed something and handed it back to Kelly. "Now you have my number. Text me your address when you get a chance. And I'll text you before I come over to make sure it's still okay."

"Um…yeah…sure…okay." *Way to look stupid.* Kelly hated that she stumbled over her words sometimes—maybe more than sometimes.

"Great. I'm so excited." Logan paused. "You probably think I'm silly getting so worked up over a cat. It's just that my place hasn't felt the same without my little guy."

Kelly didn't think it was silly at all. She'd been excited when Marley called and told her about Bear. She'd had no idea that only a short time later she would have to give him up. But Logan said she could visit, and that was important.

"It's not silly at all," Rachel said.

"It's not," Kelly said. "If you like him, I think you would give him a good home." Kelly felt her eyes well up. *Oh shit. Don't cry. Don't cry.* She swallowed hard and managed to keep the tears in check.

"Well, I better get back to work," Logan said. "I guess I'll see you tomorrow." She smiled. "Or when you need another drink." She worked her way down to the other side of the bar.

Rachel bumped Kelly's shoulder. "Oh my God. You got her phone number."

Kelly stared at her for several long moments.

"What?" Rachel asked.

"It's not like it's a date. She's coming to meet Bear. This is actually very hard for me, by the way."

"Oh, honey, I'm sorry. I know. Thirty-eight."

"What?"

"She's thirty-eight."

"She's not that much older than me. She's not an *older woman*." Kelly made air quotes.

Oh shit. It hit her that Hot Bartender—Logan—was coming to her apartment. She was suddenly very nervous at the thought.

CHAPTER TWO

L ogan put the lawn mower back in the shed and took a deep breath. There was something about mowing the lawn for the first time each season that she loved. It was exercise and you accomplished something at the same time. Kind of a two for one deal. She did lift weights from time to time but preferred useful exercise. Glad it wasn't hot enough to work up much of a sweat, she locked the shed and headed into her mother's house.

She slipped out of her grass-stained sneakers in the mud room and found her mom in the kitchen. "Lawn is done."

No matter how old she got, this was always going to be home. They'd moved into this house when she was three. The old colonial sported four big bedrooms, so she never had to share a room with her little sister, although they often ended up sleeping together in Logan's room.

Her mother handed her a glass of ice water. "Thanks, honey. Sit. Relax." She pushed her wire-rimmed glasses farther up on her nose. Her hair was just beginning to show gray at the temples, despite her being several years beyond her sixtieth birthday. She was still a beautiful woman. *Good genes*, she always said. Logan hoped she'd inherited them and would age as gracefully as her mother was.

Logan pulled out a chair from the nineteen fifties, with its metal legs and padded yellow seat. It matched the table and the other three chairs that surrounded it. It had been a wedding gift to her parents from her mom's parents. Logan had offered a few times to buy her mom a new set, but she always refused. "Why fix what's not broken?" she'd said.

Logan couldn't argue. It was in excellent shape for its age. "Anything else you need me to do before I take off?"

"Are you in a hurry? Can you stay for supper?"

"I'm going to go meet a cat that needs a new home."

Her mother pulled out a chair across from her and sat. "Are you ready for a new one? I know how hard it was for you to lose your little guy."

Logan sipped her water. She hadn't been looking for another cat, but when she heard Kelly and her friend talking, she couldn't help but ask about Bear. Maybe this was meant to be. Not a replacement cat, but a new member of the family. There was no replacing Ronald. "Yeah. If he's a good match, I'm ready. He looks like a real love."

"I hope it works out for you," her mother said. "I appreciate all the help today. There's nothing else I need done."

Logan sent a text to Kelly asking if it was still okay to come over. She said it was. Logan finished her water, put the glass in the dishwasher, and hugged her mother good-bye.

"Let me know how it works out—with this cat," her mother said as Logan headed out the door.

"I will."

Logan put Kelly's address in the GPS and was surprised it was only about a mile from her mom's house. She pointed her car in that direction and was there in short order.

She was unusually nervous as she took the stairs to the second floor of the apartment building and knocked on Kelly's door.

"That was quick," Kelly said as soon as she opened the door. She looked like she'd been crying. Those cute brown eyes were rimmed in red and her long dark hair was in a bit of disarray.

"Are you okay?"

"Yes. Why?"

Logan hesitated. "You…um…look like you've been crying. If this isn't a good time…" She turned away from the door. "I can go."

"No. No. I'm so embarrassed. Come in. This isn't easy. I was just saying good-bye to Bear." She hesitated. "Not that I'm pressuring you to take him. I mean you can. I just don't want you to think you have to." Kelly shook her head. "Sorry. I'm rambling. You probably think I'm being a baby. Only having him a couple of weeks and all."

Logan followed Kelly in. The apartment was small. The couch and TV took up most of the living room, with a small chair in the corner. What Logan could see of the kitchen didn't look much bigger. As small as it looked, it was incredibly neat. "I totally understand. It doesn't take long to get attached. We don't have to do this if you want to keep him?" She left out the fact that she would be very disappointed.

"No. I *have* to do this. I really don't have a choice. You said I could visit him. Do you still feel that way?"

Kelly seemed like a nice person. Having her come around to visit Bear would be fine—welcomed even. Other than her sister and a very occasional overnight female guest, not many people came to her apartment. Her mother had a hard time navigating the stairs, an old football injury, she would joke. But her arthritis was the real culprit. "Of course. Anytime you want."

"Be right back," Kelly said. She slipped into a room down the very short hallway. She returned holding a beautiful orange-striped cat in her arms. He was bigger than he looked in the photos.

Logan's heart opened at the sight. "Aww. He's beautiful." Big amber eyes blinked at her.

"Would you like to hold him?"

"Absolutely." Logan sat on the couch and Kelly placed him on her lap. He rubbed his head against her arm. "He's not shy, is he?"

"No. He's a lover boy for sure." Kelly sat next to them and gave Bear a pat on the head. "I haven't had any problems with him. I have a scratching post in my bedroom. He's never tried to claw the furniture."

Logan ran a hand over his silky fur. "I would love to have him. I just want you to be sure." She looked over at Kelly. She could tell how much she was struggling with this.

"I just want him to have a good home. It sounds like you can give that to him. So, I'm sure." Kelly looked like she was on the verge of tears again. "I can gather his things for you. I already put most of his toys in a bag. He loves the little fur mice. I think there might be a couple more I didn't grab yet." In an instant, she was down on her hands and knees peering under the couch, her face less than an inch from the floor and her butt up in the air.

Logan couldn't help but notice what a nice rear end it was. She forced her eyes back to the cat in her lap.

Kelly's hand shot up in the air holding two fur mice. "Here," she said. "There's one more toward the back."

Logan took them and watched as Kelly flattened out on the floor and reached under the couch. She had to admire her dedication.

"Got it," she said, her voice muffled. She popped up onto her knees, toy in hand, her hair hanging down in her face. She quickly finger combed it, only partially putting it back in place. She looked incredibly adorable.

Bear had settled right down in Logan's arm. She stroked the fur down his back as she watched Kelly.

"He likes you. He's purring up a storm." Kelly smiled.

Logan pulled her attention away from Kelly and glanced down at the cat. "He is, isn't he?" She hadn't even noticed. She'd been so intent on watching Kelly.

Kelly used the edge of the couch to pull herself up to her feet. "I got him a new litter box, so you didn't have to have a used one in your car, and there's still lots of litter in the bag."

"Wow, that was very thoughtful of you."

"It's the least I could do. I'm so grateful that you want him, and I can still see him." Kelly wiped a tear that rolled down her cheek. "I'll be right back." She disappeared down the hall again.

Logan rubbed between Bear's ears. The purring increased and he rolled over onto his back. "You certainly are a sweetheart." Logan looked up as Kelly entered the room carrying a big box, balancing a pet carrier on top. Logan hadn't even thought to bring one in her excitement to meet Bear. Kelly set everything down by the door, went back down the hall and returned with a cat tree that looked to be almost three feet tall with three levels. Apparently, Bear wanted for nothing.

It looked like Kelly had attempted to fix her hair. More of it was in place, but several strands seemed to have a mind of their own and crisscrossed where they didn't belong. "Here's all his stuff. I think the only thing you'll need to get is a new tag with your phone number. I went to get one made but the machine at the pet store wasn't working."

"Holy cow. You went above and beyond. I am so grateful. I promise to give him a good home, Kelly."

"I know you will. I can tell you two will be good for each other." Kelly put the cat tree down by the box, grabbed the carrier, and set it on the end of the couch. "Oh, and his shot records are in the box along with the paperwork from his vet visit."

"It sounds like you've taken very good care of him."

"Well, he was my baby. At least for a little while."

"He can still be your baby. He'll just live at my place." Logan wanted to make her feel better and see that smile return. She reached out and gave Kelly's hand a squeeze.

"Thank you for that."

"Of course." But Logan knew that she couldn't make it better, no matter what she said. She was serious about letting Kelly visit whenever she wanted. It was the least she could do.

"Can I say good-bye to him again, before you go?" Kelly sat on the couch between the carrier and Logan.

"Of course." Logan moved Bear from her lap to Kelly's. "Want me to give you some time alone?" She started to get up.

"No. No. You're fine."

Logan settled back down.

Kelly lifted Bear until he was face-to-face with her. "I want you to be good at your new home. I know you are going to love Logan and she is going to love you."

It was Logan's turn to tear up. She caught them in the corner of her eyes before they had a chance to escape.

"I promise to visit you as much as I can. Remember, I will always love you." She pulled him close to her chest and wrapped her arms around him. His purr was on overdrive. She kissed the top of his head and slipped him into the pet carrier. He didn't object. Kelly cleared her throat. "I'll help you bring everything down to your car," she said. "He'll be okay in the crate until we get everything else in."

Kelly grabbed the box and Logan picked up the cat tree. It looked brand new except for a bit of carpeting on one side that Bear had obviously used. They brought everything down to Logan's car in silence. Logan opened the hatch in the back and Kelly put the box in. Logan slid the cat tree across the back seat. She closed the car door and they headed back up to Kelly's apartment.

Kelly knelt in front of the pet carrier and stuck a finger in. Bear rubbed up against it. "I'll see you soon, little man." She stood, picked up the carrier using both hands, and gave it to Logan.

"Come by the bar in a day or two. I'll make you a sloe gin fizz and you can visit him."

Kelly smiled. "You remember what I drink?"

"Of course." Logan winked. She remembered what all the cute girls drank. And Kelly was certainly one of the cuter ones. "Okay? See you soon?"

Kelly nodded. She walked them to the door and quietly closed it behind them.

The carrier was heavier than Logan had expected. Bear was more muscle than fluff. She slipped it into the front seat—there was no room anywhere else—and attempted to buckle it in place. The seat belt wasn't long enough. "Guess I just have to drive extra careful," she said to Bear.

It took her three trips to bring everything up to her apartment. She set up the litter box, and food and water dishes away from each other in the half bath, while Bear explored his new home.

"Whatcha think, guy? Gonna like it here?" She picked him up and showed him where his stuff was, placing him in the litter box. He jumped out and made his way out of the bathroom. "Guess you don't need to go right now, huh? Or maybe you just don't like an audience. I don't blame you. I don't either."

If felt nice to have someone besides herself to talk to again. The place already felt less lonely. And when Kelly did visit it would be even nicer.

CHAPTER THREE

Paula looked around the apartment. "And you made sure none of his fur is still around? You vacuumed everything really good? You're sure?"

Kelly didn't know why Paula had to question her. She'd told her over the phone that she'd found Bear another home so she could come over again. That was a week ago. Paula was finally here so they could be together. "I did. There isn't any trace of him left." The statement made Kelly sad. She hadn't visited Bear in his new home yet. She thought it would be unfair to both him and Logan to do that so soon. She wanted Bear to settle in first and she thought a visit might interrupt that.

Paula looked Kelly up and down. In the past, such a move would have turned Kelly on, but she knew Paula was searching for any trace of fur on Kelly's clothes. Kelly had been very careful, washing anything and everything Bear would have come into contact with.

Apparently satisfied, Paula pulled Kelly into her arms. "I missed you. Don't be pulling any more surprises like that without asking me first." She gave Kelly a passionate kiss on the lips.

Kelly melted into her. It had been almost four weeks since they'd spent any real time together. It was her fault, she knew—and Paula was quick to remind her. She should have asked Paula before bringing Bear into her apartment.

"Let's go to bed. I have to be home by nine. Mom hasn't been feeling well and I need to check on her." She led the way to Kelly's bedroom, stripped off her clothes, and climbed under the covers. She watched as Kelly did the same.

She was so lucky to have Paula. It wasn't ideal. But Kelly knew that finding a partner when you looked like she did wasn't easy. Her mother had pounded that into her head as a child. She wasn't pretty and she was reminded often. The reminders were harsher when her mother had been drinking—which was often. But Kelly didn't blame her for trying to dull her feelings. Kelly's father left the day he found out her mother was pregnant. Kelly had never met him. She was told often that she favored him in her looks. *Unfortunate* was the word her mother used.

Paula loved her despite her plain looks and unruly hair. She couldn't ask for more than that. And she didn't.

Two orgasms for Paula later—none for Kelly, which she knew was her own fault—Paula went into the bathroom and washed up. She silently slipped into her clothes, kissed Kelly lightly on the lips, and left.

Kelly couldn't help feeling a little empty. It wasn't a foreign feeling. It happened often when Paula left right after they made love.

Kelly contemplated staying in bed and going to sleep, but eight thirty was a little early for that. She got up, slipped on her bath robe, and settled down in front of the TV in the living room. She scrolled through the channels and came upon a show called *My Cat From Hell*. She watched for several minutes in horror as Mr. Fluff terrorized the married couple that owned him, biting and scratching unprovoked.

She was surprised when tears filled her eyes and traveled down her cheeks. She wasn't sure if her sobs were for Mr. Fluff or Bear. She missed him terribly, which was just plain ridiculous. He'd only graced her life for such a short period of time. How could she have possibly become so attached so quickly?

She knew it was Logan's day off and wondered what she and Bear were doing. Was Logan out with her friends, leaving Bear alone? Were they cuddled up on the couch together watching a movie on Netflix as she and Bear had often done?

Logan had sent her a text almost every day letting her know how things were going, adding pictures to help reassure her. Bear seemed to settle into his new life with her effortlessly.

After drying her tears, she took a quick shower, stretched out on the bed, and called Logan, feeling a little foolish at her own emotions.

"Hi, Kelly," Logan said, sounding much more cheerful than Kelly felt.

Kelly wasn't sure what she had expected but this wasn't it. "Umm. Hi. I'm calling to see how everything's going and maybe…well…maybe seeing if I can come and visit Bear tomorrow?"

"Absolutely. I'm sure he would love to see you. I start work at five, but I don't have to be here if you want to come when I'm working. I can give you the key."

Kelly was surprised by Logan's generosity and trust. Her own mother never gave her a key to the house after Kelly moved out at eighteen and her mother changed all the locks. But here was a total stranger offering her that very thing. Well, not exactly a *total* stranger. But it was very kind, nonetheless.

"I'm done walking dogs tomorrow at three, if that works for you," Kelly said.

"You're a dog walker?"

Kelly was sorry she'd said that. So many people seemed to look down on her for her chosen profession. But she loved it. The dogs were great company, always excited to see her, and never judged her—unlike some of the people she'd had in her life. "Yeah," Kelly sheepishly answered.

"That's great. If I wasn't a bartender, I think that's what I would do. I love animals. You get to get all the affection without the responsibility of owning them. Have you ever had dogs?"

Kelly couldn't help but smile. Logan seemed to really understand. "I've always wanted one. My mother would never let me, and my apartment building doesn't allow them. So, I get my fix by pet sitting and walking dogs. Have you had dogs?"

"I've had a few. Growing up, my parents thought it was a great way to teach me responsibility."

"And did it?" Kelly asked. Logan was so easy to talk to.

"I think so. Even as a kid, I took it upon myself to take care of my pets. I had everything from hamsters to dogs. I always wanted a tiger, but my parents were wise enough to say no."

Kelly laughed. "Yeah. I'm thinking a tiger is going a little overboard."

"It's just a big cat."

"A big cat that can eat you," Kelly said.

"Yeah. I didn't take that into consideration. Hey, I was only eleven."

By the time Kelly was eleven she was pretty much taking care of herself. Her mother tended to drink until late into the night and sleep until at least noon, some days even later. Kelly got herself up for school, made her own lunch with whatever she could find in the house that was edible, and made sure she was at the bus stop on time. She shook the memories from her mind. Most of the time she had no trouble keeping them tucked away in the recesses of her brain. But every once in a while, they crept to the forefront.

"Kelly? Still there?"

Kelly had to think back to the last thing Logan had said. "Um. Yeah. I guess at eleven a tiger seems like a good idea."

"Right?"

Kelly wished she could talk to Logan for hours, but didn't want to impose on her time, or be a burden. "Well, I'll let you go. I guess I'll see you tomorrow."

"Great. Have a good night," Logan said.

"You too." Kelly hit the end button on her phone and tossed it on the bed next to her.

Tomorrow. She would not only get to see Bear but get to spend a little time with Logan too. Tomorrow was going to be a good day.

❖

Kelly unhooked the leash from Jack's collar. The terrier ran to his water dish and Kelly scooped a cup of kibble into his bowl. "There you go, guy. I'll see you tomorrow." She ran a hand over the soft fur on his back before leaving, locking the door behind her.

She was both excited and anxious about seeing Bear—and Logan. She tried to figure out why she was so nervous. It was Logan. There was something about her—besides her good looks—that made Kelly feel *less than*. Of course, she felt *less than* around most people. But with Logan it was even more. Not that Logan did anything to make her feel that way.

She sat in her car for a few extra minutes after pulling into the rear parking lot at Queen of Hearts. The apartment above the bar had its own entrance in the back. She took a couple of deep breaths, climbed the stairs, and knocked.

Logan opened the door, looking as good as ever, Bear in her arms. "Oh, look who's here," she said to the cat. "It's Mama Kelly. She's come to visit." She stepped back. "Come on in. He said he couldn't wait to see you."

Kelly's heart swelled, not only at the sight of Bear, but because Logan called her Mama Kelly. Logan seemed to make sure Kelly was still a part of his life.

The apartment was surprisingly big for being over a bar. In the living room the brown couch matched the brown recliner, and the coffee table matched the two end tables. It opened up to the eat-in kitchen, which sported stainless steel appliances. The whole place had a certain charm—a homey feeling. There were a set of weights in various sizes tucked into one corner of the living room, proving Kelly's theory that she must work out. No one gets toned arms like that without doing something.

Logan wore jeans with a rip in the knee and a T-shirt that was so faded, Kelly couldn't tell what it had once said. She realized she was staring in the general direction of Logan's breasts—perfect breasts—and brought her eyes up quickly.

"Have a seat," Logan said, placing Bear in her arms. "What would you like to drink? I'm afraid I don't have any alcohol. I don't drink it myself and don't have many guests."

Kelly sat on the edge of the couch and ran a hand down Bear's back. She didn't realize how much she'd missed him until now. "Anything is fine," she said.

"Soda, water, I can make coffee?"

"Soda. Whatever kind you have works."

Kelly watched Logan fix two glasses of ginger ale with ice. She set one down on a coaster on the coffee table in front of Kelly and sat in the recliner with the other.

"Has he been a good boy for you?" Kelly asked, even though she couldn't imagine him being anything other than wonderful.

"The best. He is such good company. I get done with work pretty late most nights and he's always up waiting to greet me. Of course, the fact that I always have a treat for him helps." Logan laughed. The most adorable dimples appeared in her cheeks and her eyes had that sparkle to them.

Kelly felt her face flush with heat at the sight. She was easily the most beautiful person Kelly had ever been this close to. She took a large sip of her soda to try to cool herself down. The bubbles tickled her nose, and she closed her eyes against the feeling.

"You okay?" Logan asked.

Kelly blinked a couple of times. "Yes. Just bubbles going up my nose." She looked down at Bear, avoiding Logan's eyes.

"Oh, I hate when that happens. By the way, I don't have a drinking problem. Most people assume I'm in recovery when I tell them I don't drink."

"I didn't think that. The only time I ever drink besides an occasional glass of wine at home, is when I'm out with Rachel. And then two is my limit. My mom had a problem, so I'm well aware of how much is too much."

"I'm sorry to hear that. Is she in recovery?"

Kelly brought her eyes up to Logan's, trying to gauge her true interest. Most people talked just to hear themselves. Logan seemed different. She seemed genuinely interested.

"I'm sorry. I don't mean to pry. It's none of my business. We can talk about something else if you want."

"No. No. It's okay. She died, I'm sure her heavy drinking played a major part in that. My childhood wasn't the best. Alcohol seemed to be the priority over me."

"I'm so sorry. I seem to be saying that a lot. But I really am," Logan said.

"It's okay. It was a long time ago." Kelly thought about it for a minute, doing the math in her head. "It's been almost ten years."

"And your dad?"

"Never knew him. He took off before I was born."

"Geez, I seem to be asking all the wrong questions here. Feel free to tell me to stop at any time."

Bear climbed off of Kelly and settled down next to her. He stretched out one paw and laid it across her lap.

"I love when he does that," Logan said. "Like he has to be touching you all the time."

"Me too. And your questions are fine. I got over it all a long time ago. What about your family?"

"My mom still lives in the same house I grew up in. She has arthritis so I try to help her out as much as I can. My little sister…well, not so little now…is married and works full time. She lives a few miles from Mom but is so busy with her husband and her job that it's hard for her to help out much. But I don't mind helping. It kind of makes me feel good. Ya know?"

Kelly didn't know. She couldn't imagine having that kind of relationship with her mother. She moved out as soon as she turned eighteen and rarely visited. She couldn't take the constant criticism.

"My father died two years ago."

"My turn to say I'm sorry," Kelly said. "That must have been hard."

"It was. Still is sometimes. My parents were married for forty years. I can't imagine losing a partner after that long."

The fact that Logan had used the word partner instead of husband, didn't go unnoticed. She and Rachel had speculated about Logan's sexuality but hadn't come to any definite conclusion. She wanted to ask but had no idea how to go about doing that without actually asking outright. And there was no way she was going to do that.

"Do you have siblings?" Logan asked.

"No. It was just me and my mother." *Mostly just me.*

"I'm glad I have my sister. At least the pressure was off me to provide grandkids. She is on my sister's case constantly about that." Logan laughed again. That laugh that went straight through Kelly and landed squarely on her heart—and possibly lower.

"Not a fan of kids?" Kelly managed to ask, even though she was sure nothing would come out when she opened her mouth.

"Oh no. It's not that. Just not sure if it's in the cards for me. My last relationship…let's just say she left my heart in pieces. I'm not sure I ever want to do that again."

She. She! Guess that answered that question. Kelly wasn't sure if that made her feel better or worse. "I get it," Kelly said.

"Tell me about your girlfriend."

Kelly wondered how Logan even knew about Paula, then she remembered that Rachel had said she had to find Bear a new home because her girlfriend was allergic. "Her name is Paula. We've been together for about eight months." She wasn't sure what else to say. They didn't do much other than hang at Kelly's apartment.

"It's going well then? Other than the cat allergy?"

Of course, it was going well. Otherwise, Kelly wouldn't be with her. Were there things Kelly would like to be different? For sure. Nothing was perfect. And *she* was certainly far from perfect herself. "Uh-huh."

Logan squinted at her. "That doesn't sound too convincing."

"Oh, no. Yes. It's going good." Kelly rushed to say. She didn't want Logan thinking otherwise. It was bad enough her friends did.

"You should bring her by the bar. I'd like to meet her."

"Sure." The chances of her convincing Paula to go to the bar with her were slim to none. Paula just didn't like doing things in public. "I don't know when, though. She's really busy. She lives with her mother and her mother hasn't been feeling well." There was enough truth in the statement that Kelly didn't feel bad saying it—almost.

"I get it. Drinks on the house if she can find the time. If the offer of free alcohol doesn't get her there, I don't know what will." Another laugh.

Stop. Stop feeling something every time she smiles or laughs. She is so far out of your league and besides, you have Paula.

"I'll let her know." She roughed up the fur on the paw Bear had across her leg. He yawned in response. "Am I boring you?" she said to him.

"I doubt you could bore anyone," Logan said.

Kelly was surprised. Not that she thought she was terribly boring, but she certainly didn't think she was all that interesting. Yet, Logan did seem genuinely interested in her. She wasn't sure how to respond to that.

Chapter Four

T ell me," Rachel said.
"Tell you what?" Kelly asked.
"You went to Hot Bartender's apartment. Spill. What was it like? What did you talk about? What was she wearing?"

"What was who wearing?" Marley asked, setting her tray of food on the table. The food court was slowly filling up around them. Marley was the manager at the Dress Junction in the mall, and meeting her friends there for lunch every other Monday was usually the highlight of Kelly's week.

Marley was almost ten years younger than Kelly and often acted her age, which was both cute and annoying. She had that bleached blond, blue-eyed look that the guys seemed to go for. She had a new boyfriend just about every month.

"Logan," Kelly filled in.

"Who's Logan? Oh, that bartender that you two are crushing on. Why do we care what she was wearing?"

Rachel threw a wadded napkin across the table at her. "Keep up here. Kelly went to her apartment. I want to know the details."

"Like a date?" Marley asked. She stirred her soda, releasing some of the bubbles.

"Oh my God. Remember I told you that Logan took Bear because *Paula* claimed she was allergic?" Rachel said, saying Paula's name like it burned her mouth.

"Oh yeah. I remember. The elusive Paula. If you hadn't met her, Rachel, I would swear she doesn't really exist." Marley turned her attention to Kelly. "Why is that? How come I've never met her? I thought we were better friends than that." She turned her lips to a pout. Sometimes her immature behavior got on Kelly's nerves, but what did she expect from someone that much younger?

"It has nothing to do with you, Marley. Honest. Paula just doesn't like being around a lot of people."

"I'm only one person. One person does not equal *a lot of people.*" She made air quotes with her fingers.

Kelly just shrugged. Her argument sounded lame, even to her own ears.

"We are getting off topic here. I want to know about you going to Ms. Hottie's apartment," Rachel said.

"Can we just call her Logan? I feel funny calling her that now," Kelly said. Now that they'd had several actual conversations it felt wrong.

"Fine. Logan."

"She's nice. Bear seems to fit in really well there."

Rachel rolled her eyes.

Kelly got the silent message. She told them what Logan had been wearing, somehow feeling like she was betraying Logan by sharing that information. "And we just talked while I visited with Bear. Her apartment is nice. Neat."

"What did you talk about?" Marley stuffed two French fries into her mouth.

"Normal stuff. About our families and such."

"Oh, babe, I'm sorry. I know you hate to talk about your mom," Rachel said.

That was true, but somehow it was okay telling Logan about her mother, not that she told her much. The full story would either send Logan running or feeling sorry for Kelly, and Kelly didn't want either of those things to happen.

"What did she say about *her* family?" Rachel continued.

Kelly was sure none of it was a secret, but she felt weird repeating what Logan had told her. "Mother and sister. Her father died a few years ago. That's about all I know. Sorry that I don't have any great revelations for you."

"I have to say I'm deeply disappointed," Rachel said.

Kelly shook her head. "So sorry. So sad. I can't help it if my visit wasn't as salacious as you would have liked."

"I'm sorry too. I want to live vicariously through you, and I can't do it with you and *Paula*."

"Stop saying that," Kelly said, a little more harshly than she'd intended.

Marley stopped moving, her burger halfway to her mouth and just looked from one of them to the other.

"Saying what?" Rachel asked. Either she had no idea what she had done wrong, or she was really good at acting innocent.

"Stop saying Paula's name like that. You don't have to like her. That's fine. But please respect the fact that she's my girlfriend. And she means something to me."

Rachel looked truly sorry. "You're right. I shouldn't do that. But there's something you need to understand. I only want the best for you, and I don't think Paula is it. You deserve better." Rachel laid her hand over Kelly's. "I won't do that anymore. Say her name like that. But I can't pretend that she's good for you. Or to you. She seems to be running the show and only around when it is convenient for her."

Kelly pulled her hand away. "I can't make you like her, but I think you're wrong." She pointed to her own face. "Just look at me."

"What are you talking about?" Marley asked Kelly, then turned to Rachel. "What is she talking about?"

Rachel shook her head. "She thinks she's ugly, which is absolutely ridiculous. I don't know where she gets this from."

"That's just crazy," Marley said. "I would kill to have your skin."

"Do you hear that?" Rachel asked. "Marley is willing to kill for your skin. That's how highly she thinks of you. What does that tell you? Look in a Goddamn mirror and see the truth." Rachel said it loud enough that several people turned and looked in her direction. She lowered her voice. "You're settling because you have a warped sense of who you are. I blame your mother for that. She planted poison seeds in your head, and you have been watering them ever since."

Kelly was speechless. She'd told Rachel about her mother in confidence. She never expected her to use it against her. Marley knew a little bit, but she'd told Rachel everything.

Rachel tilted her head and stared at the ceiling for several long seconds before bringing her eyes back down to Kelly's. "I'm sorry. I'm not trying to hurt you. You have so much going for you, but just don't see it. Sometimes I want to shake you and tell you to wake up. I love you. Almost everyone that has ever gotten to know you loves you."

"I do," Marley added.

"Why do you think differently about yourself than everyone else does?"

"I guess you're right. My mother planted that in my head and it's hard to get around it." Kelly had never admitted that part to anyone before, not even herself—that her low self-esteem stemmed from her mother. Her mother supplied the narrative and Kelly had no choice as a child but to believe her. But she wasn't a child anymore. Maybe it was worth examining—this feeling that she wasn't good enough.

"Honey, you need to try. Maybe get some help from a therapist or someone. Anyone. You need to start loving yourself the way we love you."

"I don't want to go to a therapist. I'm not that bad. I'll work on it."

Rachel raised her eyebrows.

"I promise," Kelly said. "Can we change the subject now? Marley, how is your job going?"

Marley talked most of the rest of the time they were together. She really liked her coworkers, but some of the customers got on her nerves, feeling they had the right to be rude and demand things they had no right to demand. "Whoever came up with the saying that the customer is always right was full of shit. The customer is seldom right in my opinion."

"Tell us how you really feel?" Rachel said as she gathered up her trash.

"That *is* how I really feel," she responded.

Kelly glanced at the enormous clock tower in the center of the food court. "I've got to get going. Have a dog to walk." She gave both of them a quick hug and headed out to her car.

Rachel's words bounced around in Kelly's head as she walked Toby, the poodle, around the block. She was well aware of the fact that her mother had failed her miserably. But maybe it was time to examine some of the damages she'd caused to her self-esteem. She wasn't sure what everyone else saw when they looked at her, but she'd never seen anything worth much when she'd looked in the mirror. Makeup helped, but not enough, and she didn't really like wearing it. Rachel often told her she looked great when they went out together. She didn't think Rachel would lie to her—but still—she didn't totally believe her. She had to figure out a way to change that.

❖

"I love this cat," Olivia said to Logan. He sat calmly on her lap as she stroked his back.

"I know. Isn't he the best? I really lucked out getting him." Logan set a coaster on the coffee table in front of her sister and set a glass of soda on it.

"I was surprised when Mom told me you got him. I didn't think you would ever get another cat after losing Ronald."

Logan sat next to Olivia. "Why?"

"Because you were so heartbroken."

She had been. Not that she'd really gotten over it. She still missed him. "It was lonely here by myself."

Olivia looked at Logan. "Oh, come on. I would be willing to bet you don't spend too much time alone."

True, there was a time when she could have put in a revolving door for all the women who came for a night or two only to be replaced by the next woman in line. But that was less than fulfilling. She still had the occasional one-night stand, but it was no longer a habit. "You'd be surprised."

"What about the woman that you got Bear from?"

"What about her?"

"Tell me about her. Why did she give this big boy up?" She raised the cat to her face and kissed the top of his head. He rewarded her with a loud purr.

"Her girlfriend is allergic. She hated giving him up. But I told her she could visit. She's come by once so far."

"Do you like her?"

"Sure, she's nice." And damn cute.

"Do you *like* like her?"

"What the hell, Olivia? She has a girlfriend."

"That doesn't mean you can't like her. I wish you would find somebody."

Why was it that people who were happily married always wanted everyone else to be married too? The last thing Logan wanted was a relationship. She'd been burned by her cheating girlfriend—partner—five years ago. She didn't want that kind of heartache ever again. "Not going to happen. Besides, I'd never get involved with someone in a relationship. Not into cheating. At all."

"I'm not suggesting you go after her if she's committed." Olivia shook her head. "Or that you go after her at all. Just be open to the possibilities with her or anyone that may come your way."

"Come my way?"

"You know what I mean."

"I do and that's why we are changing the subject. When are you and Daniel going to have kids?"

"Hey. It's bad enough Mom asks me that all the time. Don't you start on me too."

"Just trying to give you a taste of your own medicine. How do you like me sticking my nose in your life choices?"

"Message received. I won't mention…what's the name of the woman that owned Bear?"

"Kelly." Kelly. Cute Kelly. Sweet Kelly. Kelly with the girlfriend Kelly.

"I won't mention Kelly…or any other woman…or you dating…or you getting married…or—"

"I get the point. You'll mind your own business." Logan sipped her soda.

"Something like that." Bear crawled off Olivia's lap and onto Logan's. "I guess that's his opinion too. He must like his mommy being single."

It wasn't that Logan wanted to stay single. She just didn't feel like she could trust a woman with her heart again. She pulled her phone from her pocket and looked at the time. "I have to be at work in twenty minutes. Do you want to come down for a drink?"

"I would love to, but I have to go home and make dinner. Daniel's parents are coming over." She rolled her eyes.

"Tell me again how wonderful it is to be in a relationship," Logan teased her.

"It is as long as it's just him and me. His mother is so interfering. She drives me crazy."

Logan cleared her throat, loudly.

"Are you comparing me to my mother-in-law?"

"If the shoe fits…"

"If the shoe fits don't kick you in the ass with it?"

Logan gently removed Bear from her lap, rose, and set him on the couch. "You have the weirdest sayings," she said.

"Yeah, but it just makes you love me more."

"Okay. We'll go with that theory. I need to change for work. You gonna hang for a few more?"

"Yeah. I'll keep Bear company and then I'll walk down with you."

Logan only took a few minutes to change into her work clothes—black dress pants and a black button-down shirt. She slipped a thin white tie around her neck and tied a perfect Windsor knot. The tie rarely stayed on till the end of her shift. She put on a tiny amount of eyeliner and blush and headed back to the living room. "Ready."

At the bottom of the stairs, she gave Olivia a hug and let herself in the back door. She grabbed her apron from her locker, tied it around her waist, and took her place behind the bar.

She nodded hello to Helen, the young woman who covered the early shift and overlapped with Logan's for several hours. She was surprised to see Kelly and her friend walk in. What was her name? Robin? Rachel? Something like that. They sat at the bar on the side Logan covered.

"Are you here to gin and Bear it?" she said to Kelly. "Get it? Gin and Bear it."

Kelly laughed. "That was—"

"Cheesy. I know," Logan offered.

"I was going to say cute. But yeah. Cheesy fits too." Kelly's smile lit up her face. "Gin yes. Bear no. I don't feel right visiting him when you're not there. And you're here, so obviously you're not there." The blush creeping up her neck landed squarely on her cheeks. "That was a pretty lame thing to say."

Logan was quick to reassure her. "Hey. If I can be cheesy, you can be lame. We'll call it even." She laid her hand on top of Kelly's and was surprised at how soft it was. Must be great genetics or one hell of a moisturizer.

"I'll take a—" Rachel started.

"Old-fashioned," Logan finished for her. She may not be great at remembering names, but she sure as hell remembered what her customers drank. "And sloe gin fizz for you, Kelly?"

"Yes, please."

Logan set about making the drinks and set them in front of them. She put her hand up when Kelly tried to hand her money. "Drinks are on the house tonight."

"You can't do that."

Logan laughed. "I can and I will. Besides, I know your limit is two drinks, so I probably won't go broke paying for it."

Kelly couldn't believe Logan had remembered that. "Thank you. I appreciate it," Kelly said.

"Me too." Rachel held her drink up.

"How have you been, Kelly? Bear was asking about you," Logan said.

She had a way of putting Kelly at ease. "You can tell Bear that I've been great. Picked up two more clients this week."

Logan leaned her arms on the bar. The move brought her face closer to Kelly. Kelly could see the tiny amount of makeup she had on, proving that Logan had a natural beauty that didn't need to be enhanced. Logan was so close that Kelly could smell—was it her shampoo or some kind of body spray—strawberry vanilla. She was momentarily flustered.

"Dogs? What kind?" Logan asked.

"What?"

Logan stood, creating more space between them. Kelly was both relieved and disappointed.

"Your new clients. Do they have dogs?"

"Oh. Oh yeah. Two more dogs to walk. German shepherds. And when their son is in town they asked if I would walk his dogs too." She found Logan so easy to talk to—when she wasn't so close to her.

"I think you're being paged." Rachel nodded in the direction of a couple who were seated a few barstools away.

"Thanks," Logan said and went to wait on them.

"She is so darn hot," Rachel said once Logan was out of earshot.

"She's so darn nice," Kelly added. Calling her hot all the time just didn't seem right anymore. She noticed Rachel was staring at her. "What?"

"Nice?"

"Yes. She's very nice. I like her." Kelly's phone vibrated in her back pocket, startling her. She was surprised to see it was Paula. Kelly hit the answer button. "Hi, honey."

"What are you doing? I was thinking of coming over for about an hour," Paula said.

"I'm at the Queen of Hearts bar with Rachel. Why don't you come and join us?" She turned away from Rachel. She didn't want to know if she made a face or worse, pantomimed throwing up.

"Babe, you know I don't like bars. Can you meet me at your apartment in ten minutes?"

Shit. She was torn between rushing home and staying out. It was early still. She knew that if she left, Rachel would be pissed and if she didn't, Paula would be. It was a no-win situation. She glanced up in time to see Logan heading back toward them. Damn. She really wanted to stay and talk to Logan more as well.

"Kelly? I'll see you in ten minutes." Click.

Kelly pulled the phone away from her ear and stared at it in her hand.

"What's going on?" Rachel asked her.

"Paula wants me to meet her at my apartment. In ten minutes."

Rachel opened her mouth to say something, but Kelly cut her off. "Don't say it."

"You don't even know what I was going to say."

"You were going to say, Fuck Paula. Stay here," Kelly said.

"I guess you did know exactly what I was going to say."

"I've gotta go."

Logan got to them just in time to hear that. "Going so soon? You haven't even finished your drink."

"Yeah. She was ordered to go home," Rachel said.

Kelly gave her a look that said *shut up.*

"Ordered?" Logan asked.

Kelly struggled for the words to explain without making Paula sound like a bitch. "My girlfriend…"

"Ordered her to go home," Rachel said.

"She didn't order me," Kelly said, even though she kind of did.

"Um…okay," Logan said. "Hey, listen, Kelly. I was wondering if you wanted to come over for dinner on Wednesday. You could visit Bear and I'm a great cook, if I do say so myself. And I do." She smiled and Kelly's heart melted a little at the sight. "You would be doing me a favor. I don't usually get a chance to cook for company and I kind of miss it."

Kelly hesitated. Visiting Bear for a little while was one thing. Having dinner with Logan was a whole other thing.

"You can think about it and let me know," Logan said.

"Okay. I'll text you." Kelly took a big gulp of her drink. "I'm so sorry, Rachel. I promise I'll make it up to you."

"It's okay." She gave Kelly a hug. "I just want you to be happy. I love you."

"Love you too," Kelly said. She gave a quick wave and headed out the door.

Kelly walked in her apartment door fifteen minutes later. "Hello," she called out.

Paula's car was in the parking lot. She had a key, so Kelly assumed she'd let herself in.

"I'm in the bedroom. And you're late."

Kelly found Paula in her bed. "I've only got a little while. Hurry up," Paula said.

They had sex—it didn't feel like making love—and Paula went into the bathroom to clean up, like she always did after they'd been intimate. She emerged from the bathroom fully dressed.

"I was thinking of seeing a therapist," Kelly said, trying to make conversation and thus keep Paula there longer.

"Why bother paying someone?" Paula asked. "I can list everything that's wrong with you for free."

That wasn't the response Kelly was expecting. She was at a loss for words.

"There are too many things to get into now. I've got to get going." Paula kissed Kelly on the top of her head and left.

Kelly was stunned and she felt used. Like any body would have been sufficient for Paula. She wished she'd done the one thing she never did with Paula. She wished she'd told her no. She slipped out of bed, pulled her robe on, and dug her phone out of her pants pocket that she'd deposited on the floor.

I would love to have dinner with you on Wednesday, she texted Logan. She wondered if Rachel was still at the bar or if she'd gone home after Kelly abandoned her. She was too embarrassed to call or text her to find out. She hadn't been a very good friend, leaving like that. She wasn't sure if she was madder at Paula for pushing her around or at herself for letting her.

She tied the belt around her robe and settled down on the couch in front of the television and mindlessly scrolled through the stations, stopping on an old rerun of *Friends*.

Her phone pinged announcing she had a text.

It was from Logan. *Excellent! Does six work? Anything you won't eat?*

She typed out her response. *Six is great. Not crazy about fish or olives. Anything else is fine.* She started to feel better and looked forward to dinner with Logan—probably much more than she should have.

CHAPTER FIVE

Kelly hadn't talked to Rachel since she'd left her at the Queen of Hearts bar two days earlier. She owed her an apology. She also expected one in return. It was so unlike her to call someone out on something they said or did. But she was getting sick of being treated poorly by her friends and especially by Paula.

She started her car and pointed it in the direction of Logan's apartment. "Call Rachel," she said into her Bluetooth.

Rachel answered on the second ring. "Hi there."

"Hi. First, I want to say I'm sorry for leaving the other night. I know now that I shouldn't have done that."

"Okay. I wish you hadn't."

"The other thing I want to say..." Kelly let her words drift off. She wasn't sure how to phrase it. "Um...I don't appreciate that you told Logan that Paula ordered me to go home."

"Yeah, but—"

"There is no *but* here. You made me look like an idiot. Please don't do that again." Kelly's heart was racing, but the stress it caused to call Rachel out was worth it.

"You're right. I'm sorry. I shouldn't have done that."

Well, that was easier than Kelly thought it would be. She was prepared to state her case and tell Rachel how it made her feel. She briefly considered still spelling it out but decided that would be overkill. "Thank you."

"Are you heading over to Logan's? Did you decide to have dinner with her?"

"I am."

Rachel was silent for several beats and Kelly could almost hear the wheels turning in her head. Kelly figured she was deciding whether to say something derogatory about Paula or something positive about Logan—and how hot she was.

"I'm glad," Rachel responded, surprising Kelly. "I hope you have a nice time. And you get to see Bear. I know that will make you happy."

Wow, Kelly thought. "Thank you. I appreciate that. Drinks tomorrow night? My treat."

"Are you offering to make up for deserting me the other night?"

"I am."

"Then I accept," Rachel said.

"Can I ask you a question?"

"Of course. You can ask me anything."

"Why did you suggest that I see a therapist? Are there all kinds of things wrong with me? I mean, I know there are, but are there *a lot* of things?"

"That's exactly the point. There is nothing wrong with you, but you think there is. Of course, you aren't perfect. You're human. We all come with built-in flaws. But you seem to have exaggerated yours. And totally believe things that aren't true about yourself."

"Like what?"

"Like you're ugly. My friend, you are beautiful, inside and out. But you look in a mirror and you see the ugly reflection that your mother pushed on you."

"But—"

"Stop. You just don't see what the rest of the world sees."

Kelly listened to the words Rachel was saying but had trouble absorbing them. How could the reflection she saw in the mirror not be the truth?

"Don't get mad at me for saying this, but that's why I don't want you with Paula. She is just feeding your feelings of worthlessness. She isn't good enough for you."

Paula wasn't good enough for her? She'd often thought the opposite. If she had been good enough for Paula, then surely Paula would be willing to be seen with her in public. If that didn't tell Kelly that she was worthless, then she didn't know what did.

"Kelly?"

"Huh?"

"I want you to be happy. I don't think you can be truly happy until you learn to love yourself. That's why I suggested the therapist. Do you think it's something you're willing to do?"

"I don't know."

"Will you at least think about it?"

It was pretty much all she thought about since Paula said she had a list of faults. She wanted to find out what that list was so she could try to change. Then maybe Paula would really love her.

"Will you?" Rachel repeated.

Kelly had been so lost in her thoughts she'd forgotten that Rachel had asked her a question. "Yes. I'll consider it."

"Good."

Kelly pulled into the back parking lot of Queen of Hearts. "I'm here. I'll see you tomorrow."

They said their good-byes and Kelly hung up. She'd been so in her head about her faults, Paula, and the possibility of therapy that she hadn't even allowed herself to get nervous about having dinner with Logan. That changed in an instant as acid flooded her stomach.

One more thing to add to the list. *I apparently can't even have dinner with a gorgeous woman without getting sick to my stomach.* She swallowed back the bile that was rising in her throat.

She grabbed the paper grocery bag from the passenger seat and headed up the stairs. Logan answered the door almost as soon as Kelly knocked.

"Hey you. Come on in." Logan stepped back to let Kelly pass. "You look great and what is that incredible smell?"

She's just being nice, Kelly thought. "I made stuffed mushrooms." She held up the bag.

"Nope. I don't smell mushrooms. It must be your perfume." Logan sniffed the air surrounding Kelly. "I'm guessing honeysuckle."

Kelly wasn't used to someone, other than maybe Rachel, noticing how she smelled. Or looked for that matter. Paula certainly didn't. "It *is* honeysuckle. You're very observant." Kelly held up the bag again. "I also brought a few cat toys for Bear." She looked around the room, more out of a need to break the intense eye contact she somehow seemed to be having with Logan, than to actually look for Bear.

"He was lying on the bed in my room a few minutes ago. Feel free to get him. It's the first door on the right." Logan pointed down the hallway.

Kelly felt weird at the thought of going into Logan's bedroom but did as she was told. The room wasn't what she expected. The flowery bedspread was made up of mostly pink hues, matching the soft pink walls. Three full-sized, framed movie posters graced the walls. All three were from sci-fi movies. Several books were sprawled across the nightstand. The top book looked like a romance, but Kelly didn't venture far enough into the room to know for sure. The long dresser was littered with a variety of things, a small lamp, hairbrush, hand lotion, and a couple of bobble heads that Kelly didn't recognize but must have been from some space movie, judging by the uniforms they were wearing. She was still surveying the room when Bear, stretched out on one of the pillows, let out a loud yawn.

"Hey there." She stepped over a pair of sneakers by the side of the bed and sat down, running her hand over Bear's orange fur. "I've missed you."

"I see you've found him." Kelly jumped at the sound of Logan's voice.

"Sorry. Didn't mean to startle you."

"It's okay. I'm just a stupid wimp. Sorry."

"Don't do that," Logan said.

Kelly started to get up. "Oh. I'm sorry. I shouldn't have sat on—"

"No. Sit. That's not what I mean. Don't put yourself down like that. You aren't stupid, or a wimp."

Kelly wasn't used to someone defending her from herself. She was at a loss for words. "Okay," she finally managed to squeak out. She searched her brain for something else to say. "Um. Who are the figures on your dresser?" Lame.

"This one"—she picked up the female figure—"is Captain Janeway from *Star Trek Voyager*. And this guy is Captain Picard. He was later promoted to admiral." She shook her head. "I know. I know. I'm a nerd. I freely admit it."

"How come you get to call yourself a nerd, but I get in trouble for calling myself a wimp?" That didn't seem right.

"Because a nerd isn't a bad thing. A wimp sounds so negative. You are anything but a wimp. Or anything else negative for that matter."

It was one thing for her friends, who loved her, to tell her she was wrong about herself, but here was someone who was practically a stranger telling her the same thing. Maybe there was something to this after all.

"You okay?" Logan asked.

"Yes. Why?"

"You just looked lost in your own head there for a minute. I hope I didn't hurt your feelings."

"No. You didn't. I was just…no…never mind."

Logan sat on the bed next to her. Close to her. Deliciously close. Too close. Kelly found it hard to breathe with her that close. When Logan placed her hand on top of hers, Kelly thought she might just pass out from the intensity of it. Paula. I have Paula, she reminded herself. Stop feeling what you're feeling.

"Just what?" Logan asked.

Kelly had lost track of their conversation. "What?"

"You started to say something about being lost in your head and then stopped. I'd like to know what you were going to say."

Kelly considered making something up, but the last thing she wanted to do was lie to Logan. "Why are you so nice?" she asked.

"Okay. You don't have to answer. I didn't mean to pry." Logan started to get up, but Kelly grabbed her hand and pulled her back down.

Kelly stared into those beautiful green eyes. The sudden impulse to kiss Logan shocked her. "I was going to say that my friends have been telling me that I don't think enough of myself. So, you saying basically the same thing kind of...I don't know... kind of made me think maybe they're right." Kelly couldn't believe she'd just shared that. But there was something about Logan—something beyond her beauty and killer body—that made Kelly want to be close to her. To tell her things. To bare her soul.

"Thank you for telling me. I think your friends are right. I know I haven't known you long, but I think you're a great person. I'm getting the feeling that you don't think the same."

"I had it pounded into my head since I was born that I'm a burden. A mistake. It's hard to get past that." She had known Rachel for a couple of years before she'd admitted these things to her. And she still hadn't told Marley much about her childhood. But here she was telling Logan. "When I look in the mirror all I see are the flaws. The problems. The person who isn't worth loving."

Logan wrapped an arm around Kelly's shoulder. "Oh, honey, your mother was so wrong."

Kelly got lost in the comfort of Logan's closeness for several long beats. When she'd told these things to Paula, her response had been, "we've all got childhood shit." The fact that Logan had called her *honey* didn't escape her attention, either.

"How do you know?" Kelly asked.

"Because I can tell. You're good people. I think being a bartender for so long has given me superpowers." She laughed. "I can tell if someone is a good person or a shmuck before they even open their mouths. I can spot the cheaters, the honest people looking for a partner or a date or the person just trying to get out of the house and away from a spouse for a while."

Kelly tilted her head and looked at Logan out of the corner of her eyes. "Really?"

"Really. I don't know if it's a blessing or a curse."

"And how did you know I was *good people*, as you put it?" No one had ever told her that before.

"It's in your eyes. They're kind. And when you told me you walk dogs, I knew for sure. Only kind people would do something like that. You never see old, grumpy people doing that job. It takes someone caring and gentle. You took Bear in when he needed a home. You gave him up, even though I could tell it broke your heart because that's what was best for your girlfriend. That takes love."

Love. She'd always thought she loved Paula. But she was wondering if it was more desperation than true feelings. More than that, she was doubting Paula's love for her. She rarely said it anymore. In fact, Kelly couldn't remember the last time Paula had said those words. How come Paula couldn't be more like Logan? Then there would be no doubt of her feelings—or Kelly's feelings for her. "Thank you for saying that."

"It's the truth. One thing you can always get from me is the truth. Honesty is important to me." There was a hint of sadness in her words.

Kelly wasn't sure if she should ask why or not.

"I was engaged once. She cheated on me. Of course, with the cheating there were plenty of lies. I promised myself I would never let myself be put in that position again. So, yes, honesty is important to me. And relationships, beyond friendship, are not an option. Not anymore."

Kelly wasn't sure why, but that revelation disappointed her. Not that she was looking to have a relationship other than friendship with Logan. Or was there a small part of her that was wishing that? No. That would just be stupid. Even if Logan was looking for a girlfriend, Kelly was sure she wouldn't fit the bill. She just wasn't on the same level. And she was sure she never would be.

"I'm sorry. That must have been hard."

"It was. Thanks. Back to you for a minute. Your mother was an honest person?" She asked.

Kelly didn't even have to think before she answered. "Not at all. She said all kinds of shit that wasn't true."

"Then why did you believe her when she put you down?"

"I…" Kelly didn't have a good answer. She didn't know why.

"Do you think she knew you? Really knew you?"

Again, the answer was immediate. "She didn't know me at all. She never bothered getting to know me." Kelly had accepted the fact that her mother was terrible. She thought she'd gotten over it a long time ago. She was surprised when she found herself close to tears.

"Let's look at the facts here. Break it right down to the bare bones. Your mother didn't know you and she didn't always tell the truth. Yet you believed her when she told you that you were less than. Not good enough. Seems like you still believe it. Why do you think that is?"

Kelly wiped a stray tear from the corner of her eye. "I'm not sure. I guess because there wasn't anyone telling me otherwise."

"No one?" There wasn't an ounce of pity in Logan's voice. It was filled with compassion.

Kelly's thoughts ran through her childhood. There were teachers who were kind to her, and childhood friends. But their voices were never louder than her mother's. "I guess there were some people that were kind to me and believed I was okay."

"Well, you can add me to that list. I think you are more than just okay. A lot more."

Kelly resisted the urge to wrap her arms around Logan and pull her into a tight hug. Apparently, Logan didn't resist the same urge. Before Kelly knew what was happening, she was in Logan's embrace.

Kelly felt good in her arms. Too good. She had a girlfriend, Logan reminded herself. Besides, she wasn't looking for anything more than friendship from Kelly. She was too good to be one of her one-night stands. All she wanted to do in that moment was comfort her. She'd been handed a raw deal in life—a mother who sucked and no father at all. No wonder she had self-esteem issues. Who wouldn't?

"Mmfursher," Kelly said into Logan's shoulder.

Logan pulled back enough to look into Kelly's eyes. "What?"

"I said thank you."

"You don't have to thank me. That's what friends are for."

"I'm sorry I'm such a—"

"Watch it," Logan interrupted her.

"Umm. A good hugger. Yeah, that's it. I'm sorry I'm such a good hugger. Most people find it annoying what a good hugger I am."

Logan laughed. "Good save. You *are* a good hugger, but I'm afraid if I don't stop hugging you now the meatloaf is going to burn, and I don't want to feed you burnt meatloaf." She reluctantly took possession of her arms back. Kelly really was a good hugger. She was a lot of good things. She just needed to believe in herself more. "Hey," Logan said. "Want to toss the salad for me? I'll bet you toss as good as you hug."

Kelly laughed and Logan warmed to the sound of it. "Sure. But I haven't tossed much in my life, so keep your expectations low."

"Low expectations on the tossing. Got it." She stood, grabbed Kelly's hand, and pulled her to her feet. She didn't let her hand go until they were in the kitchen. "Salad contents are in the veggie drawer in the fridge. Everything's washed." Logan grabbed a bowl from the cupboard. "Cutting board and knives are to the left of the fridge."

"Hey. You said I was tossing. Not making the whole salad," Kelly said with a smirk.

"First you cut. Then you toss. It's all in the salad-making manual. It's around here somewhere." She pretended to look around. "Now where did I leave that?"

"You're funny," Kelly said. "I like you."

"I like you too. And I like that you think I'm funny. I would have liked it more if you said I was hilarious, but I'll settle for funny." Logan watched as Kelly opened the refrigerator and peered into the vegetable drawer.

"If you say something hilarious, I'll be sure to let you know."

"Deal." She set about checking on the meatloaf while Kelly gathered the salad fixings. It wasn't long before everything was done, and they set the table together. "It's so nice to have company to share a meal," Logan said. "I eat alone so much of the time."

"I find that hard to believe," Kelly said. "Um. I mean I don't think you're lying. It's just…umm…I mean…" It was adorable the way she was stumbling over her words.

Logan rested her chin on her hand, elbow propped up on the table. "What is it that you mean?" She watched a blush creep up Kelly's face.

"It's just that you are so beautiful, you must have women chasing after you all the time."

"Oh, I do. But I don't let them catch me." She smiled. "I'm very picky about who I give my time to. My free time is precious to me."

"Yet you let me come here and visit Bear and you even invited me to dinner."

"My point exactly." She meant it as a compliment and had no worries that Kelly would think she was flirting with her. After all, she had Paula. "I am content to have my family and a few good friends. I'd rather have four quarters than a hundred pennies."

"Al Capone."

"What?"

"That quote. It's from Al Capone."

"It is not."

A smile lit up Kelly's face. "It is. You can google it. The whole quote is, *be careful who you call your friends. I'd rather have four quarters than a hundred pennies.*"

Logan was impressed. "How do you know that?"

Kelly shrugged. "I just know stupid...umm, I mean, I know a lot of trivia. It's sort of a hobby."

"A woman of many talents. We should enter a trivia contest together. I know a lot of nerdy, science fiction stuff. I can name all the characters on *Wynonna Earp* and the actors' names, as well as all the Star Trek, Star Wars, and...well you get the point."

Kelly finished the last bite of food on her plate. "I don't know anything about sports. Do you? You look like you probably played something or other. Volleyball or..." She squinted at Logan and tilted her head. "Or at least softball."

"Would you believe me if I told you I was the quarterback on my high school football team?"

Kelly's eyes widened. "You were? That's so cool."

Logan rose and stacked Kelly's empty plate on top of hers. "I wasn't. I just wondered if you would believe me."

Kelly tapped the table. "I thought you were always honest?"

"I am, except when I'm kidding. I'm a kidder. Did I fail to mention that?"

"As a matter of fact, you did fail to mention it."

"I didn't play any sports in school. I was trying to hide the fact that I was a lesbian and figured sports would just draw attention to it. Besides, I hate sports. Playing them, watching them, thinking about them." She piled the silverware on top of the plates and deposited them into the sink.

"When did you come out?" Kelly asked.

"College. Hard to hide being gay when you have a real live girlfriend. You?"

Kelly seemed to think about it for a few moments. "Not sure I ever officially came out."

Logan stopped midway on her return trip to the kitchen, a plate of meatloaf in one hand and a bowl of leftover mashed potatoes in the other. "You're not out?"

"I'm out. I guess I just never made an official announcement. I never really talked about it to my mother. She didn't seem to like me anyway. I think telling her I'm gay would have widened the divide between us. My friends just seemed to know." She paused. "Thinking back, I'm not sure how they knew. I didn't have my first girlfriend until my mid-twenties. Late bloomer, I guess. It didn't last long."

"How come?" Logan rinsed the dishes and handed them to Kelly to load into the dishwasher.

"Guess she didn't like me enough to stick around. I haven't had much luck with women. I always figured it was because of the way I look."

"I think you look damn cute." It was the truth, plain and simple. Not meant to be flirtatious. "Anyone who can't see that is a damn fool."

Kelly wasn't sure if Logan was flirting or telling her the truth. Not many people, other than Rachel and Marley, had ever commented on her appearance. She didn't respond, even though saying thank you crossed her mind. She just shook her head.

Logan wiped her hands on a dishtowel, put a hand on each of Kelly's shoulders, and turned her around, facing the direction of the living room.

"What are you doing?" Kelly asked.

"I want to show you something." She gently pushed until Kelly was walking. Logan steered her in the direction of the bedroom and for a moment Kelly panicked. As much as she liked Logan and she was sure sex with her would have been wonderful, she had Paula to consider. She wasn't a cheater.

Logan directed her past the bed and into the adjoining bathroom. Kelly wasn't sure if she should be relieved or disappointed. Logan stopped when Kelly was in front of the sink and thus in front of the mirror. "Tell me what you see."

Kelly began to object and turned away from the mirror. The last thing she wanted to do was look at herself.

Logan turned her around again. "Please," she said. "Humor me."

Kelly could see her hair was a mess, her eye liner wasn't completely even, and every other flaw that made up her face. She wasn't sure what Logan expected her to say.

"Okay. Let's start with your eyes. What do you see?"

"I think they are too far apart. And the color is dull."

Logan shook her head. "Kelly, no one else in the whole world sees that when they look at you. Those brown eyes are beautiful. The color is deep, there are little flecks of gold in them, and they hold kindness. They also hold a certain sadness. I think that was put there a long time ago by a woman who never understood your worth."

"My mother?"

"Your mother. She did you a great disservice. And did you know that the space between your eyes usually equals the length of one of your eyes?"

Kelly shook her head.

Logan opened a drawer in the sink cabinet and pulled out a tape measure. "Hold still."

Kelly held her breath as Logan, only inches from her face, measured one of her eyes and then the space between them. She was so close that Kelly could feel the warmth of Logan's breath on her cheek. She wanted to close her eyes and breathe in the essence of her but knew that wouldn't be a good idea. For one thing it was rude to close your eyes when someone was trying to measure them. She laughed out loud at her stupid thoughts.

"Why are you laughing? Your eyes are the perfect distance apart, by the way. I know this is crazy, but I wanted to prove to you that you're wrong about the way you see yourself."

"At least now I can add another bit of trivia to my collection, about the space between your eyes…err, my eyes…umm, anyone's eyes."

"True story. I learned that in one of my art classes."

"You took art classes?" Logan was full of surprises.

"I did. But this is about you."

"What kind of classes?"

Logan turned Kelly back toward the mirror and stepped behind her. She was a couple of inches taller than Kelly, and Kelly could easily see her in their reflection.

Logan had a hand on each of Kelly's shoulders. Kelly could have easily melted into the warmth of them—into the warmth of Logan.

"Want to know what I see when I look at you?"

Kelly looked at Logan's reflection. Her breath caught in her throat and all she could do was nod.

"I see a heart-shaped face with strong cheekbones, perfect skin, a bow-shaped mouth with a slight pout to it when you aren't smiling, and the cutest cleft in your chin."

Kelly brought her eyes to her own reflection. She never would have described herself that way.

"Doesn't your girlfriend ever tell you how beautiful you are?" Logan asked.

Kelly looked away. Afraid to catch Logan's eye. She simply shook her head. Paula never told her she looked nice. Never commented on her appearance at all. Sure, she paid her compliments when they first started dating, but never about her looks. Kelly tried to remember the last time Paula had complimented her at all. She couldn't come up with an answer.

"Well, damn. What's wrong with her? Is she blind? Or stupid?" Logan grimaced and covered her mouth with her hand. "Oh shit. I'm so sorry. I shouldn't have said that. My bad."

Kelly turned toward her. "No worries. Paula isn't—well, Paula isn't, let's say very demonstrative. But she's so good to me in other ways." She prayed that Logan wouldn't ask her what ways, because she'd have a hard time coming up with an answer.

"I'm just trying to get you to see your own worth here, Kelly. Not that looks make someone a good or bad person. But if you're wrong about your appearance, what else are you wrong about? Your intelligence? Your personality?"

"I don't know. I just never thought I had much to offer someone."

"That's just crazy. You have a lot to offer and anyone you choose to be with is very lucky. I'm gonna tell Paula that if I ever meet her. Want me to call her right now and tell her?" Logan raised her eyebrows and smiled. "'Cause I will." She pulled her phone from her pocket. "What's her number?"

"You're insane. You know that?"

Another smile. "I do. I think it's one of my best features."

"It is. I adore your insanity," Kelly said. She realized there were a lot of things about Logan that she adored, but it would be best to keep them to herself. She decided it was something she wouldn't even share with Rachel, and she told Rachel just about everything.

"Why don't we go find Bear and you can cuddle with him on the couch while I finish cleaning up the dishes? Then we can find a movie on Netflix for the three of us to watch. Bear is a big Sandra Bullock fan, but I think he's watched just about every one of her movies we could find. So, let's not let him pick out the movie."

"Yep. Insane you are. Is that how Yoda would say it?"

Logan laughed. "You've been holding out on me. You know Star Wars."

"I've never seen any of them, I just know Yoda talks funny. Object, then subject, then verb. It's just more of my useless trivia."

"How dare you? Nothing about Star Wars or Yoda is useless. Useless nothing is."

"Okay then. Lesson learned."

"I should hope so. Let's go find Bear."

The dinner, the movie, the company—especially the company—was perfect. Kelly hated to see the evening end. The good-bye hug Logan gave her at the door made Kelly momentarily weak in the knees. She thought that was just a cliché, something they talked about in romantic comedies, but apparently it could really happen. She needed to get a grip on her feelings—or was it her libido—before she said or did something stupid.

Her apartment felt extra empty and very lonely as she flipped on the lights. She had the urge to call out *hello,* just to see if it would echo back.

Logan had given her a lot to think about. She'd basically said the same thing Rachel had been telling her, that she had the wrong impression of herself, and her low self-esteem was unfounded. But Logan had done more than just lecture her. She made Kelly look at herself. Really look. Kelly tried to see herself through Logan's eyes, and when she did, she didn't seem quite so unattractive.

She knew she would never be as beautiful, kind, or witty as Logan. Not many people could be that great. But maybe she could stop thinking of herself in such a negative way. There were people who liked her, even cared about her. So she couldn't be that bad of a person. Right? And the dogs she walked were always happy to see her. Animals had a sixth sense about them. They knew who they could trust to take care of them. They knew *good people* as Logan had phrased it. Maybe her mother was wrong about her. She'd been wrong about everything else.

Kelly had just slipped into her nightshirt after brushing her teeth and washing her face when her phone pinged with a text. She expected to see Rachel asking her how dinner had gone. She was surprised to see it was from Paula. Paula never texted her this late. She said she didn't want to be distracted in case her mother needed her. Rachel had said it was a lame excuse, but Kelly thought it was kind of Paula to care about her mother so much. They obviously had the kind of relationship Kelly wished she'd had with her own mother.

"I have a couple of hours of freedom tomorrow evening while my mother's friend is visiting. I'll be over about six." Kelly read the text out loud, a lame attempt to not feel so alone. It didn't help.

"Well, at least she wants to see me when she has time," Kelly said to no one. She started to type out a response and stopped.

Yes. Of course, I would love…

She remembered she had plans with Rachel to make up for deserting her the last time Paula beckoned her. She erased what she had written.

Sorry. I can't. Plans with Rachel.

She waited for Paula's response, hoping she would understand. But no response came. Kelly crawled into bed, placed her phone on the nightstand so it would be close by in case Paula answered, and closed her eyes. But sleep eluded her. Jumbled thoughts of Paula, and how angry she must be that Kelly had said no, mixed with thoughts of Logan and what a great time they'd had together. Logan. Kind, beautiful, wonderful Logan.

Logan was the last thing she thought about before sleep finally overtook her. She hadn't been asleep long when she woke with a start. Thoughts about Logan had turned into dreams about Logan. Dreams of Logan's lips on hers. Logan's hands on her, and in her. She reached between her legs to where her blood was surging and was surprised at how wet she was. She closed her eyes and finished where her dream had left off, imagining her own hand was Logan's. It was a fantasy she knew would never happen, so there was no harm in exploring it in her mind and letting her body have what it so desperately wanted. But it wasn't her body she was worried about. It was her heart.

CHAPTER SIX

"W e've been sitting here for fifteen minutes, and you haven't once asked me about dinner with Logan or said anything bad about Paula. Are you okay?" Kelly asked Rachel. She adjusted herself on the tall barstool and sipped her drink.

Rachel let out a quiet laugh and nodded in Logan's direction, who was making a drink for someone at the other end of the bar. "I wasn't sure you wanted to talk about it with Ms. Hot—I mean Logan, so close by. And as for Paula, you know how I feel. There is no sense rehashing it. Besides, you told me to respect your relationship with her and I intend to honor that." Rachel fished the cherry from her glass and popped it into her mouth, extracting the stem in one swift movement.

"I appreciate that. I want you to know that Paula wanted to come over tonight and I told her I couldn't because I was hanging out with you." Kelly still hadn't heard back from her, even though she'd sent her three more texts apologizing for not being available. If there was one thing Kelly hated, it was someone being mad at her, especially Paula. That seemed to be happening more and more lately.

Rachel stared at Kelly, eyes wide, for several beats before she responded. "You did? I'm glad and frankly, a little shocked."

"You were right. I let her push me around too much. It's time I stood my ground." Although that ground felt very shaky.

"Good for you. I'll bet she didn't like that," Rachel said, but was quick to add, "Sorry. I didn't mean that as an insult."

"I don't think she did. But I can't keep letting her call all the shots."

Rachel raised her glass and clinked it against the glass in Kelly's hand. "Amen to that, sister."

"Amen to what?" Logan asked as she approached them, wiping her hand on the small towel tucked into her waist band.

Kelly was sure Rachel would say something negative about Paula in that moment, but she didn't. "Amen to girls' night out," Rachel said. "Among other things. Like standing up for what you believe in."

Logan laughed that laugh that made Kelly's stomach clench and she pressed her thighs together against the sensation that was starting to stir.

"And what do you believe in?" Logan asked.

"I believe I'll have another drink?" Kelly answered. She looked down at her half full glass. "As soon as I finish this one."

"By the way," Logan said. "Bear said to tell you he really enjoyed spending time with you yesterday."

"Bear did, huh?"

"Okay. I'm paraphrasing. He actually meowed, but I surmised that he had just as nice a time with you as I did."

Kelly couldn't help but smile. "I had a really nice time too."

"Then we'll have to do it again sometime. Soon."

"How about I cook next time?" Cooking was a life skill Kelly learned early for her own survival.

"Deal."

Kelly caught Rachel staring at Logan, mouth half open. She ignored it until Logan went to make drinks for the couple several seats over and was out of earshot. "What, Rachel? You couldn't seem to keep your eyes in your head," she said.

"Did you see the way she looked at you?"

"What are you talking about?"

"I don't know. It's hard to describe. But something's different. She doesn't look at anyone else in here like that."

"You're being ridiculous. We're friends. She wasn't looking at me any differently than she would any other friend." There was no way Logan was looking at her as anything special.

"I'm telling you that she was."

"Drop it, Rachel. Please." Kelly was having enough trouble containing her thoughts—and libido—when it came to Logan. She didn't need Rachel planting seeds of hope that didn't exist. Besides, she had Paula. Paula who hadn't bothered answering a text in almost twenty-four hours. Kelly was beginning to do something she almost never did. She was starting to get really pissed at her. She was tempted to tell Rachel about her feelings but thought that would just give Rachel more reason to dislike Paula.

They spent the next few hours chitchatting about pretty much nothing. Logan joined them from time to time but never stayed for more than a minute or three before someone flagged her over to get a drink.

Logan wished she could have spent more time with Kelly and Rachel, but it was a busy night and she had lots of drinks to make. Kelly seemed to be a little distracted, like something was scratching at the back of her mind. Logan didn't feel she knew her well enough to ask if there was a problem, at least not in front of Rachel. She wished she did.

The evening seemed to drag once Kelly and Rachel said their good nights and were on their way. All Logan wanted to do was finish her shift and go upstairs to cuddle with Bear. She wasn't one to feel lonely, but for some reason she felt alone. She briefly considered taking the blonde at the end of the bar up on her offer to show Logan a good time, but she knew it would only add to her lonely feeling in the long run.

It was a little after two in the morning when Logan climbed the stairs to her apartment. She'd left a lamp and the radio on for

Bear, although she wasn't sure if he cared one way or the other. She changed out of her work clothes, slipped into the old T-shirt she slept in, and scooped Bear up in her arms.

It often took her at least an hour to settle down enough to go to sleep after work, so she turned off the radio and settled down with Bear in front of the TV. She flipped through the channels without really paying attention to what was on. She couldn't get Kelly out of her mind, and she wasn't sure why. What was it about Kelly that drew her in? She was cute, kind, funny, interesting. But so were a lot of people she knew.

She lowered the volume on the television when she thought she heard her phone ringing from the bedroom where she'd left it when she changed out of her clothes. Who would be calling her at this time of night? It wasn't her sister's or her mother's ringtones that she had programmed into her phone. She wondered if it was a wrong number or some emergency. She scrambled down the hall to answer it. She was surprised to see it was Kelly calling and her heart sped up a few beats.

She was slightly out of breath as she answered. "Hi, Kelly. Are you okay?"

"Oh my God, did I wake you? I thought you would still be up seeing as you just finished your shift."

"No. No, I wasn't sleeping. Everything all right?" she asked again.

"Yes. I couldn't sleep and…well, I guess I just wanted to chat. Is that okay?"

"Absolutely. I was just thinking about you. I must have manifested this phone call." She wasn't sure she should have admitted that. And wasn't sure why.

"Ahh. The law of attraction. You should think about the winning lottery numbers and see if you can win a jackpot."

A phone call from Kelly felt like she had already won. "I guess that means I would have to actually play the lottery." Logan piled her pillows up, sat down on the bed, and leaned against them. Bear jumped up next to her.

"Not a gambler?"

"Not really. Seems like I lose when I gamble." She absently stroked the cat's fur, and he rewarded her with a loud purr.

"Talking about anything in particular?"

Logan hesitated before answering. "Love."

"Oh wow. I wasn't expecting that answer. So, you aren't willing to gamble on love?"

"Been there. Done that. She stole the T-shirt."

"I'm so sorry." Logan could hear the sincerity in Kelly's voice.

"I survived." Just barely.

"Can I confess something to you?"

Logan's stomach dropped. She thought for a minute Kelly was going to confess feelings for her. If Kelly went there, Logan wasn't sure how she would respond. If she was being honest with herself, she had growing feelings for Kelly, but she sure as hell wasn't going to tell her that. "Umm. Sure."

"I'm starting to question my relationship with Paula."

Logan tried to hide the sigh of relief she let out. "You aren't happy?" Lame question, she told herself, but she wasn't sure what else to say. She ran her fingertips over the paw that Bear stretched across her stomach.

"She wants me at her beck and call and gets mad when I'm not. But she is only available to me when she feels like it. Rachel doesn't like her and I'm beginning to see why."

"How about your other friends? What do they think of her? Sometimes friends can see stuff we can't when we are all caught up in the emotions of a relationship."

"That's part of the problem. None of my other friends have met her. She doesn't ever want to go out or get together with my friends, or hers, for that matter."

That didn't sound like the basis for a healthy relationship. Logan needed to tread lightly. If she badmouthed Paula and Kelly decided to stay with her it could put a wedge between them. The last thing she wanted was to lose Kelly as a friend.

"What do you think, Logan? Be honest with me. I know it's not normal, but is it terrible?"

"I think you need to ask yourself why she doesn't want to go out in public or meet your friends."

"She said she wants to be alone with me. I thought maybe she was embarrassed of me."

"Well, that's just bullshit." Logan cringed at her choice of words. "I mean that doesn't make sense, Kelly. Any woman would be proud to have you on their arm." I sure would, she thought, but didn't dare say. "Let's take that reason off the table. Now what other reason could she have?" Logan suspected she knew the answer, but wanted Kelly to figure it out, not to be cruel, but she figured if Kelly came to her own conclusion she couldn't blame Logan if it was the wrong answer. It was probably the coward's way out.

"Maybe because she doesn't want word to get back to her mother that she's gay. Her mother is a homophobe. But it's not like we would make out in public. And that wouldn't explain why none of our friends can come over." Kelly was silent for several beats. "Do you think she has a partner she's cheating on?"

Bingo! "That's a possibility."

"Oh shit. Oh shit. Oh shit. That makes the most sense, doesn't it?"

Logan couldn't stand the thought of the pain that would cause Kelly. But if that was the case, better Kelly find out now.

Kelly wasn't sure what to think anymore. Was it possible that Paula had been lying to her the whole time? She felt sick to her stomach. What a fool she had been.

"Kelly?"

"I'm here," she managed to squeak out.

"Talk to me. What are you thinking?"

"That I'm an idiot." Only a fool would have believed Paula's lies for almost nine months. Nine months of her life wasted. She had only herself to blame. No. She wasn't to blame. Paula was to blame. If this was true. There was still doubt in her mind. Maybe she was wrong. Maybe Paula was shy or an introvert or—or—or. Kelly didn't want it to be true.

"You are not an idiot. Don't say that." Logan's words cut into her thoughts. "Do you think you can find out? Maybe ask her?"

"If she is cheating with me and has a wife or worse yet, a husband, I don't know if she would tell me."

"Maybe you could try googling her?"

"She's not on social media, so I don't know what I would find."

"I'm pretty good with this stuff. I could help you if you want."

"Help me what? Find out the truth?" It was suddenly too much for Kelly to absorb.

"Yes. I could help you find out if she has a significant other." She paused. "If you want. I don't mean to pressure you."

The last thing she thought Logan was doing was pressuring her. Yes. She needed to know the truth. All she could do was hope it wasn't true. "Please. That would be great."

"What time do you start your dog walking in the morning?" Logan asked.

Kelly shook her head trying to think. Tomorrow was Friday. She didn't have any morning clients on Friday. "Noon."

"How about we get together at nine or ten? We could meet somewhere with internet for breakfast, or you can come here, and I'll make omelets. Either way we can use my laptop."

"I can come there. But I doubt I'll want to eat." She wasn't sure she would ever want to eat again. "Wait. You worked late. Isn't that early for you to be up?"

"That doesn't matter. I just want you to have peace of mind, one way or the other."

Kelly wasn't sure anyone had ever treated her so kindly. "Are you sure?"

"Yes. Just tell me what time?"

"Ten?"

"Okay. Kelly, I know it's none of my business, but you deserve to be treated better than Paula seems to be treating you."

Kelly couldn't argue with that. Paula was great at the beginning, but not so much lately. Sometimes she even bullied Kelly. Kelly always seemed to make excuses for her. Maybe it was time to stop and look closely at the relationship for what it was. Kelly needed to figure out what exactly *that* was.

"I hope I haven't overstepped here," Logan said. "I just care about you."

"No. I really appreciate your input."

"Why don't you try to get some sleep? If you can. We can figure this out in the morning. Kelly?"

"Yeah?"

"You're going to get through this. I promise."

Kelly wasn't sure how, but she believed Logan. "Thank you. I'm sorry I called so late."

"No worries. I'll see you in the morning. Okay?"

"Okay. Bye and thank you."

Kelly hit the *end* button on her phone and set it on the nightstand. Her head was swimming. She had too many thoughts floating through her brain to land on any that might help her figure this out.

Rachel had been telling her for months that Paula didn't treat her right. But Kelly had chalked that up to the fact that Rachel didn't like her. Logan had just told her the same thing. She did deserve better. She'd never even considered that before. It was time to kick the sound of her mother's voice telling her that she wasn't good enough out of her head. Logan was right. Her mother hadn't really known her. So, her opinion of Kelly didn't count. In fact, her opinion was worthless, just like her role as a mother.

Was Paula just as worthless?

CHAPTER SEVEN

Logan hit the snooze button on her alarm clock for the third time. She'd had a hard time falling asleep after her phone call with Kelly the night before and four hours of sleep definitely wasn't enough. Fifteen minutes later, she was standing in her shower with warm water splashing over her, willing herself to shake off the feeling of exhaustion.

She was on her second cup of coffee when Kelly knocked on her door.

"I'm not really sure I want to do this," Kelly said as soon as Logan let her in.

"We don't have to do anything you aren't comfortable with. Come in. Coffee?"

Kelly nodded. "Please." She followed Logan into the kitchen.

"Milk, sugar?" Logan asked as she poured the last of the coffee from the pot into a cup. "I've got vanilla creamer in the door of the fridge you can grab if that is more your style."

"That would be great," Kelly answered. Logan watched her as she helped herself to it as if she'd been in Logan's life forever. Logan liked that she was comfortable enough to do that.

They settled down across from each other on the couch.

"Does it matter if Paula is married?" Kelly asked.

Hell, yeah it does, Logan thought. "Don't you want to know the truth? Do you still want to be with her if she's got a significant other?"

Kelly shook her head. "Maybe that's the point. I don't think I want to be with her at all. I've been making excuses for her behavior for a long time. Even to myself. I'm starting to realize that I do deserve better." She sipped her coffee and let several long beats go by before continuing. "There's still a part of me that believes I don't deserve to be treated better than Paula treats me."

Logan started to object, but Kelly held up her hand, stopping her.

"I know that is ridiculous. I do. But changing my thought pattern overnight just isn't going to happen. It's a process. A process that begins with telling Paula it's over."

"Is that what you want?"

"No. What I want is for Paula to be single, totally into me, and to treat me right. But that isn't going to happen. So, ending it is my only option."

"Oh, Kelly, I'm so sorry." A plethora of emotions flooded through Logan. Sadness for what Kelly was going through. Relief that Kelly would be out of that horrid relationship. Happiness that Kelly would be single. Wait. What? It didn't matter if Kelly was single. They were friends. Nothing more. If she truly wanted Kelly to be happy, and she did, then it would make sense that it didn't matter if Kelly was partnered or single as long as Kelly was content. "What can I do to help?"

"You've already done it. You've opened my eyes to something I should have seen a long time ago. You know, it's funny, Rachel has been telling me for a while that Paula wasn't good for me or to me for that matter. I never really listened to her. I don't know why. You talk to me once about it and it all becomes clear."

"Why do you think that is?"

Kelly shook her head. "I'm not sure. There is just something about you that…" She hesitated.

Logan wasn't sure whether to push her to answer or not.

Kelly cleared her throat. "I mean, I know Rachel cares about me and wants the best for me. But with you, it feels different." She shook her head again. "I'm sorry. I'm not making much sense."

"I care about you too. I hope you know that," Logan said.

"I do. That's what I'm trying to say. I guess. I'm sorry."

"Stop apologizing. I know what you're going through isn't easy." Logan's heart had been ripped out of her chest and stomped on by a cheating ex. She knew how painful breakups were. "I'm here for you. Whatever you need."

"Why are you being so nice to me?" Kelly asked.

The question threw Logan. Why wouldn't she be nice to Kelly? Kelly was worth being nice to. Anyone who couldn't see that was an idiot. "Because you're a great person who deserves the best."

"Thank you." She got up, set her coffee cup on the kitchen counter, and turned to Logan. "I'm going to go and let you go back to bed. You look tired." Still beautiful, but she clearly didn't get enough sleep.

"What are you going to do now?"

"Text Paula. Ask her to come over and have a talk with her. It's not something I'm looking forward to, but it has to be done." She paused. "Tell me I'm doing the right thing."

Logan rose and closed the gap between them. She pulled Kelly into a tight hug. "You're doing the right thing," she whispered, close to Kelly's ear.

Kelly closed her eyes against the rush of feelings that coursed through her. She liked Logan's arms around her—way too much. She pulled back far enough to look into Logan's eyes. "Thank you," she said. "I really appreciate you listening to me."

"Anytime." Logan walked her to the door, gave her one more hug, and said, "Call or text me later and let me know how you're doing."

Kelly nodded. "I will." She made her way down the stairs to her car and sat there for several long minutes staring at the phone in her hand.

She typed out a text to Paula. *Can you come over please? Tonight, if possible. Please.* She had no idea if Paula would even answer. She was halfway home when her phone pinged with a new text. She was tempted to pull over to read it but convinced herself it could wait until she was safely in her own parking lot. Her stomach did a series of gymnastic moves that made her feel sick. She pulled into her parking space and read the text.

Why should I come over when you totally rejected me? Paula responded.

I would like to talk about that. Please come over.

You owe me an apology.

Paula wasn't going to make this easy. Maybe I should just break up with her via text, Kelly thought. *I'm sorry.*

That's all you have to say?

Kelly's frustration turned to anger. *What more do you want me to say, Paula?*

Well if you don't know then that is on you. You're the crazy one.

What the hell did that mean? Kelly was done. There was no sense begging Paula to come over so she could do this face to face. *I'm over this. I'm breaking up with you.* There it was. She said it. There was no taking it back now. Kelly felt like she was going to throw up.

You don't get to decide that. Paula typed back. What the hell? Paula couldn't stop her from breaking up with her.

YES. I DO.

Great. Fine. You were never worth the risk anyway.

Kelly was more confused than ever. *What does that mean?*

It means you're too stupid to figure out that you were my side piece. I wasn't even allergic to your crappy cat. My wife is. She would have killed me if I came home with fur on my clothes. So you got rid of him for nothing. Poor little you. All alone again. Good luck finding anyone as good as me. Fuck you Kelly!!!!!

Kelly was sure she was going to vomit. She had been right. Paula had been cheating with her. She had been using her all along. And Kelly had bought it, hook, line, and sinker. And that sinker was heavy enough to pull Kelly under.

She pounded her fists on the steering wheel hard enough to cause a sharp pain in the side of her hand. She hit it a couple more times trying to increase the physical pain enough to dislodge the pain in her heart. It didn't work.

She told herself not to cry until she was in her apartment. That didn't work either. She met her neighbor Sam coming out the main door as she was going in.

"Hey, Kelly," Sam said. "How are you doing?"

Kelly burst into tears.

"Oh wow. You okay?"

Kelly shook her head. She was in no shape to talk. She slipped past him and hurried up to her apartment. She closed the door behind her, leaned against it, and slid down to the floor. With her face buried in her hands, she sobbed uncontrollably. She wasn't sure how long she'd sat there but knew she wasn't all cried out. She also knew she had to get ready to start her dog walking jobs for the day.

She pulled herself up, blew her nose and washed her face, grateful for the fact that the dogs wouldn't care if her nose was red and her eyes looked glassy. Her head was swimming as she drove to her client's house. How could she have been so stupid? There were so many clues that she'd missed. It wasn't a homophobic mother Paula was hiding her from. It was a wife. She had a fucking wife. The words that bounced around Kelly's head threatened to set off another round of sobs. She managed to keep it under control until she was halfway around the block with Duke the Doberman. She swiped at the tears as they rolled down her cheeks. She wasn't sure if she was angrier at Paula for fooling her or at herself for believing all of Paula's bullshit excuses.

Her mother was right. She did lack the intelligence God gave an ant. Damn Paula. Damn her mother. They were both pieces of shit that proved to be nothing but heartache for Kelly. She didn't need either one of them. She didn't need anyone.

Duke pulled ahead of her, straining the leash and her arm as they neared his house. Kelly deposited the poop bag in a garbage can in the garage as they made their way in. She made the dog sit as she poured food into his bowl. He leaped at it, sending some of his kibble flying, as soon as Kelly gave the signal that he could eat. He had the whole bowl and the stray pieces on the floor eaten before Kelly was even out the door.

The rest of the day went pretty much the same. Walking, crying, feeding, more crying. Her phone pinged with a text just as she pulled into the parking lot of her apartment building. Her stomach lurched with the thought that it might be Paula. She was relieved to see it wasn't.

It was from Logan. *Thinking about you.* Short. Simple. Caring.

For a moment, Kelly's heart swelled. But only for a moment. Thoughts of Paula invaded her brain again. She considered answering Logan's text but didn't know what to say. She wasn't ready to admit to anyone just what a fool she'd been.

She pocketed her phone and made her way up to her apartment, grateful that she didn't run into any of her neighbors this time.

Her stomach objected to the thought of eating anything for dinner. She slipped into her sweats, flopped down on the couch in front of the television, and scrolled through Netflix stopping on a Sandra Bullock movie, *Unforgivable.* The name of the movie seemed appropriate for her current situation. Besides, Logan said that Bear liked Sandra Bullock movies so that fit her mood as well.

She continued with depressing movies for the rest of the evening, ignoring several texts, not caring who they were from. She left her phone on the end table in the living room when she went to bed, positive that it would be futile to try to sleep. A day's worth of crying had tired her out more than she realized. She fell asleep right away and didn't wake until morning.

Her eyes felt like they were coated with sand as she blinked them open. It took her a minute to realize what day it was and the fact that she didn't have any dogs to walk. She tried to take weekends off, but sometimes she worked when her clients went out of town or otherwise wouldn't be home. She was thankful that wasn't the case. She considered staying in bed, but her bladder had other ideas.

After a quick trip to the bathroom, she padded to the kitchen and peered into the refrigerator. She wasn't really hungry and wondered if she would ever be able to eat again. She ignored the pings from her phone. Whoever was texting her could wait until she got herself together.

The shower she thought would help, didn't. She was afraid only time would—but she wasn't even sure about that. What was that saying? Time heals all wounds. She hoped that time wounded all heels as well. Then that heel Paula would get hers. The anger Kelly had felt the day before came roaring back.

How dare she? Paula was a liar, a cheater, a bully, and all-around asshole. The part that angered Kelly the most was she knew she would miss Paula. At least the Paula she knew at the beginning of their relationship. Relationship? Kelly wasn't sure that was the right word anymore. Affair. That was closer to the truth. And Kelly played the unwitting part of the mistress.

Wasn't it the mistress that was supposed to be treated well? Wasn't she the one that got the flowers and jewelry and all the best attention? Paula couldn't even follow the rules for having an affair. Thinking back, Kelly realized that it was only the first couple of months that Paula treated her kindly. It got progressively worse the longer they were together.

Well, fuck her and the horse she rode in on. She wasn't worth the time or tears Kelly was shedding. The fresh round of sobs was for herself. Not Paula. She deserved to cry for her wasted time. Wasted love. Wasted trust.

Another text message notification rang out. Kelly reluctantly retrieved her phone and realized she had fifteen missed texts messages.

Four were from Rachel.

Hey there! How are you doing?

Haven't heard from you in a while. Everything ok?

Give me a call or at least text me back when you get this.

Ok. Now I'm getting worried. Where are you?

The three from Marley were similar to Rachel's.

The rest of the texts were from Logan. She was also worried that Kelly hadn't answered any of her texts. The last one said that she was going to stop over to make sure Kelly was okay if she didn't hear back from her.

As much as Kelly looked forward to seeing Logan under normal circumstances, all she wanted was to be alone. She sat on the couch and typed out a group message to all three friends.

I'm sorry I worried you. I broke up with Paula yesterday. I don't want to get into the details right now. I'm still processing them. I've learned lately that life comes at us and through us in cycles. Cycles of good times. Cycles of bad time. Cycles of everything else in between. I seem to be in one of those bad cycles. Some things feel hard. Some things feel impossible. Nothing feels particularly good right now.

She paused to gather her thoughts and figure out the best way to phrase what she was feeling.

Think of me like a flower bulb in the cold, hard ground. All around me seems dark and bleak. But I know better than that.

Know that this time of being dormant and seemingly nothing is just a phase in a cycle. The sun will be back. Please don't think I don't care or want to be with you. That's not the case. I'm asking you to be patient. Thank you for caring about me.

She reread what she wrote. Satisfied, she hit send. In less than a minute she had a reply from all three of them.

I'm so sorry my friend. I'm here for you, Rachel texted.

Wow! That's hard stuff. No wonder you want alone time, Marley said.

Know that I care about you. Whatever you need, you got—time alone, time with friends, time with Bear. Please take care of yourself while you start to heal. You deserve so much in life, Kelly. Don't ever forget that. Logan's text brought a fresh round of tears. How could someone as great as her care about someone as insignificant as Kelly felt? Kelly smiled at that thought, knowing that Logan would reprimand her for thinking it. She took a minute to reformulate it.

"I'm very blessed to have friends who care about me," she said out loud.

❖

Wow, Logan thought. That text showed the depth of Kelly's intelligence as well as the depth of her pain. Breakups were painful, no matter who was doing the leaving. At least Kelly didn't live with Paula so she wouldn't have to deal with dividing everything and finding another place to live, like Logan had to do when her last relationship broke up.

She had no choice but to wait for Kelly to see the sun again and come back around. She just hoped it wouldn't take her long. She sat on the couch and swooped Bear up into her arms. "We need to send positive energy to Mama Kelly, big guy. What do you think? Can you help me with that?"

He yawned in response.

"Does that mean you aren't going to do it, or that you don't think she'll need it 'cause she'll be just fine?" She set him down next to her and stroked his fur. He laid one paw across her leg. "Yeah. You're right. She'll be fine. She's a strong person. She just doesn't know it. She doesn't know just how great she is."

Logan felt restless and wasn't sure why. It wasn't like she saw or even talked to Kelly every day. So, why did not being in communication with her now feel weird. Somehow empty. She shook her head. It didn't make any sense.

She wanted to help Kelly through this and at the same time respected her need to be alone. Thoughts of Kelly ping-ponged through her brain. The sound of her ringing phone brought her out of her head, making her jump and Bear leap off the couch.

She grabbed it off the coffee table and answered it without looking at the caller ID hoping it was Kelly. "Hello."

"Hello. We have an amazing offer for you—"

Logan hit end. "Damn telemarketer." She threw her phone on the couch next to her. "What the hell is wrong with me today?"

She opened the drawer on the bottom of the coffee table and pulled out her drawing pad and pencils. She didn't draw too often but found it to be a welcome distraction when she did. Bear had settled down on the chair across from her. The perfect subject.

She drew in the basic shapes that made up the orange cat and slowly added more details in until she had captured his essence. Instead of drawing the chair underneath him, she drew a lap. Kelly's lap. She searched her memory for the shape of Kelly's body and committed it to the paper. When she got to Kelly's face she hesitated. It wasn't that she didn't have access to every detail of it in her brain. It was that she wasn't sure she could do her justice.

Logan decided to leave the face blank and worked on the hair, including several wayward strands that often had a mind of their own on Kelly's head. She set the drawing on the coffee table and went in search of her sneakers. Maybe a walk, or better yet a run, would help clear her head and keep thoughts of Kelly at bay.

She found one in front of her dresser and the other under her bed. Five minutes later, she was outside squinting against the bright sunshine. A quick stop at her car to grab her sunglasses and she was on her way around the block. The slight breeze felt good against her face and her bare arms. She started out at a brisk walk and slowly transitioned into a full run. The faster she ran, the faster thoughts of Kelly invaded her brain. This obviously wasn't working.

She returned home, changed out of her sweaty tank top in favor of an old T-shirt, and called her sister.

"What are you doing today, Olivia?" Logan asked instead of saying hello when her sister answered.

"Daniel and I are going out on his brother's boat for the day. Why? What's going on?"

"Nothing."

"Bull. There is something on your mind. Spill."

Logan hesitated. She wasn't sure how to explain her feelings when she didn't even understand them herself.

"Logan?"

"Kelly broke up with her girlfriend and is going through a tough time," Logan said in a rush.

"And...?"

"And what?"

"And that affects you how?"

Again, Logan was at a loss for an explanation.

"Logan?" her sister repeated

"I'm thinking," she answered a little too harshly.

"What's going on with you?"

Logan paced around the living room. "I don't know. I just..." She paused. "I guess I want to figure out a way to help her through this. I know how painful breakups can be."

"Are you sure that's all there is to it?"

"No. I'm not sure," Logan said. "I'm wondering if I care about her more than I should." There. That summed it up. Didn't it?

"And how much are you *supposed* to care about her?"

Good question. "I guess as much as you are supposed to care about a *friend*. Not more than that."

"I didn't realize there was a limit to how much you should care about a friend," Olivia said.

"You know what I mean." Logan scooped Bear up with one arm as he attempted to walk past her. He put up a fuss and she set him back down. He hurried to his food dish and let out a loud meow. His dish was nearly full, but you could see the bottom of it through the pile of dry food. If there was one thing Bear hated it was not having a totally full bowl. Logan poured a little more food for him, and Bear leaped on it as if he was starving.

"You mean you like her more than just a friend."

There it was. The truth. Her sister had hit it squarely on the head. "I guess that's the problem."

"Why is it a problem? You said she broke up with her girlfriend. She's single. You're single. I say go for it."

"Don't you think that's a little insensitive? I mean she just broke up with her yesterday."

"I'm not telling you to jump her bones today. I'm just saying you can feel free to explore this and see if she feels the same about you."

Silence for several seconds.

"I mean," Olivia continued. "When is the last time you felt like this about someone? Anyone?"

Logan didn't even have to think about it. "Judith. And we both know how that ended…with her cheating and me with my heart in pieces. I don't ever want to go through that again."

"So, you think Kelly is like Judith?"

"Not at all. They couldn't be more different."

"Logan, I don't see what the problem is."

"The problem is I can't seem to get her out of my head. I don't want another relationship. With anyone. Anyone."

"Oh. I get it. You're having feelings you don't want to have. It's not that you don't want to explore these feelings. It's that you don't want to be having them."

That was it. "Yep."

"It's not like you can snap your fingers and have your feelings go away."

"Yeah. No. Not possible."

"Sounds like you have a dilemma on your hands. Want to know my opinion?"

Logan was pretty sure she knew what Olivia was going to say. "Go for it."

"I think you should stop fighting it." Yep. That's what Logan predicted. "It's not like someone comes along every day that stirs these feeling in you. I don't think it's something that you are going to be able to ignore."

"That's what I'm afraid of."

"Why afraid?"

"Olivia, I don't want to get hurt again."

"You are way overthinking this. Having feelings for someone doesn't mean you're going to get hurt. Take it day by day. Give her time to heal. Be her friend. If something more develops, don't fight it. You might just find the love of your life."

Logan scoffed at her. The love of her life? She was pretty sure that didn't exist. At least not for her.

"Or not," Olivia added. "I know you are going to do what you want to do, no matter what I say. You are bound and determined to live your life alone. Not all women are like Judith. She was a bad apple that needed to be tossed."

"True. But how can I trust anyone after what she did to me?" The conversation was going around in circles. There didn't seem to be an answer except to shove her feelings down and ignore them. That was the only logical thing to do. "Besides," she continued. "I hardly know her."

"That doesn't seem to be stopping you from liking her. Let's turn this around and talk about Kelly instead of you."

"What do you mean?"

"Tell me about her. What do you like about her?"

Logan wasn't sure she wanted to play this game. Bringing her feelings to the forefront was the exact opposite of what she wanted to do.

"Come on. Tell me."

She knew her only choices were to tell her sister or hang up the phone. There was no way Olivia was going to drop it. "Okay. Physically she's very cute. Bright brown eyes. Uncontrollable long dark hair. A very cute butt." Logan realized she was pantomiming with her hands as if she was cupping Kelly's butt cheeks. She couldn't help but laugh at herself.

"And personality-wise?" Olivia asked.

"Kind, caring, honest and not the least bit pretentious. She had a hard childhood that still seems to affect her, but she's working through that." And Logan wanted to help her get through it. To show her what a wonderful person she really was.

"She sounds like a real loser. You should run away as fast as you can."

"Olivia, you aren't helping here."

"I'm just trying to open your eyes to what's right in front of you. You don't have to chase her or marry her or whatever. You just have to be open to the possibility that she may feel the same and you may have something worth checking out. And you don't have to make any decisions today. If I know you, you're driving yourself crazy trying to figure this out and put it out of your head at the same time."

Apparently, Olivia did know her because that was exactly what she was doing.

"So, what am I supposed to do, oh wise one?"

Olivia laughed. "It's about time you realized how wise I am. Relax. That's my advice. Relax and be her friend. If something more comes out of it, don't fight it. If nothing more comes out of it, then you were freaking out over nothing."

"Is that what I'm doing? Freaking out?" That's exactly what she seemed to be doing.

"Hang on," Olivia said. Logan could hear her talking to someone else, most likely her husband. "Listen, Logan," she said. "I have to get going. Daniel is ready to go. I'm not sure what time I'll be home. Want me to call you when we get off the boat?"

"No. That's okay. Thanks for listening and the advice." The advice she wasn't sure she was going to take.

"I love you. You'll figure this out. Catch ya later."

"Love you too."

Relax. Let things happen as they will. Or not happen at all. Logan didn't know which one to wish for.

CHAPTER EIGHT

Two and a half days of wallowing and self-pity was enough. Kelly needed to get back to real life. Her friends had sent simple *I'm thinking of you* texts. But they had respected her need for alone time to process everything. She was ready to return to the land of the living.

Duke was waiting for her by the front door as she let herself in. "Hey there, big boy. Ready for your walk?"

He did a happy dance, mostly by wiggling his butt uncontrollably, and whined. Kelly clipped the leash to his collar, and out the door they went. Nothing cheered her up like the greetings she got from each dog as she opened their doors for their walks.

She set a bowl of fresh water down for Pringle, her last dog for the day, gave him a pat on the head, and locked the door behind her. She called Rachel on her way home and filled her in on the details of her breakup.

"Oh geez. I'm so sorry. I knew Paula wasn't any good for you, but I had no idea she was that bad."

"Live and learn I guess," Kelly responded. It still hurt, but there was also a freedom in dumping Paula that she hadn't expected to feel. She no longer had to jump when Paula said jump or feel used when Paula left right after they'd had sex. Now she knew the reason she'd done that. She needed to rush home to her little wife she was cheating on. What a piece of shit she turned out to be.

"What can I do to help?" Rachel asked.

"Nothing. Just knowing you're there for me helps. I'll get through this."

"I know you will. What are you going to do now?"

"Like right now?" Kelly asked.

"Like right now. Like tomorrow now. Like next week now."

"I was thinking of stopping by the Queen of Hearts and talking to Logan, see if maybe I can go up and see Bear for a while. I have to tell you it stings that I gave him up for a stupid, fucking, shit-face liar."

"Wow. You shouldn't sugarcoat it like that. Tell me your true feelings."

Kelly laughed—and it felt good. "Shall I add bitch, asshole, and the C word to my list?"

"She was definitely the C word, and I don't mean cute."

"Can you do me a favor and fill Marley in on what happened? I would rather not rehash the whole thing with her, but she deserves to know."

"Of course."

Kelly pulled into the Queen of Hearts parking lot. "I'm at the bar. I'll text you later."

They said their good-byes and Kelly hung up. She took a deep breath and went inside. It took several seconds for her eyes to adjust from the bright sunlight to the fluorescent glow inside.

The place was nearly empty, way too early for the evening rush. There was a couple at one of the tables and two guys with an empty stool between them at the bar. Logan had her back to her, rearranging some of the liquor bottles on the back shelf. Kelly eased herself onto a barstool. "What's it take to get a drink around here?" she said loud enough for Logan to hear her.

Logan turned, bottle of vodka still in her hand. "I guess that depends on who's asking."

"Umm. That would be me asking."

Logan's smile lit up her face. Kelly was sure the smile she returned was just as wide.

"I'm so glad to see you," Logan said. She lowered her voice even though Kelly doubted that anyone was close enough to hear them. "How are you doing?"

"I'm alive. It was a close call there for a day or two. Thought maybe a shattered heart would do me in."

Logan placed her hand on top of Kelly's. The gesture went straight to Kelly's heart and set her libido on fire. Without Paula to think about she no longer felt guilty for her body's reaction. She knew Logan only meant it as friendship and Kelly knew it would never amount to more, but she figured it would do no harm to enjoy the feelings it stirred.

"I'm so sorry you have to go through this," Logan said.

"You were right. Paula has a wife that she was cheating on. And get this…" Kelly paused. The words were harder to say than she thought they would be. "She's not even allergic to cats. Her wife is. So going home with fur on her clothes would have been a problem."

"Holy shit. No."

"Yep." Kelly knew how attached Logan had become to Bear. As much as she would have liked him back there was no way she would do that to her.

"She told you that?"

"Through texts. Yeah. I wanted to break up with her in person, but she pushed me…bullied me really…that I felt forced to do it that way. I think she told me that as a way to punish me. Tell me how stupid I am. Was."

"You know that's not true, don't you?"

"I was stupid to believe her lies."

"Love makes us do stupid things. It doesn't mean you're stupid."

"I've had a few days to think about this now. I'm not sure I was really in love with her. I think I was with her out of desperation."

One of the men at the other end of the bar cleared his throat loudly and held up his glass. "Hold that thought," Logan said. "Be right back."

All Kelly had done since breaking up with Paula was think. She had hardly eaten anything and hadn't even showered until that morning. She'd walked around like a zombie trying to sort out her feelings. She'd concluded that she'd clung to Paula because she thought Paula was her only option. Well, if Paula was the best she could do then she was better off alone. She could beat herself up emotionally just fine. She didn't need Paula, or anyone else for that matter to do it for her. If no one else came along and she stayed single for the rest of her life she could be okay with that. At least she wouldn't be walking on eggshells anymore, scared that one wrong move could cause disaster.

The disaster she'd worried about happened—okay, she made it happen—and she didn't die. Didn't sink into a black hole of despair. Didn't even cry after that first night.

"You were saying?" Logan asked as she approached. She set a drink down in front of Kelly. "Sloe gin fizz."

Kelly was touched. Why couldn't she find someone as nice and caring as Logan was? She took a sip of her drink. "What was I saying?"

"You said you weren't sure you were ever in love with Paula."

"Oh yeah. She seemed so into me at first. I thought maybe I'd found the one. I guess I ate up all the attention. But once she had me, she changed. I held on hoping she would change back. Now I know she never would have. I was more in love with the idea of love than with Paula." She tilted her head. "Does that make sense?"

"Perfectly. Sometimes it takes pain to help us see things clearly."

"Well, that just sucks."

Logan laughed that laugh that made Kelly lightheaded. "It does. But that's how we grow stronger. A tree that never gets swayed by the wind never grows a strong bark and thick trunk."

"Are you saying I'm getting a thick trunk?" Kelly smiled.

"Your trunk is perfect just the way it is...as is the rest of you." Logan pulled a glass out from under the bar and filled it with soda water. She held the glass up. "To your perfect trunk and your happiness. You've got this."

Kelly felt a little weird toasting to herself. "And to good friends," she said and clinked her glass against Logan's and took a drink. "Thank you."

"For what?"

"Being there for me. Making me feel better about myself. For a million little things...that aren't so little to me."

"I didn't do anything except care."

"And that, my friend, means the world to me." She held her glass up again.

Kelly never did get around to asking Logan if she could visit Bear. She was content to chat with her until the bar filled up around them and Logan was swamped filling drink orders. "I'm going to get going," Kelly said when there was a slight lull. "Thanks again for everything."

"What are you doing this Wednesday?" Logan asked.

"I have dogs until three, then nothing."

"How about we go out to dinner and a movie? Help take your mind off things."

Things. Paula things. It would be great to take her mind off stupid Paula things. And Logan was the perfect person to help her with that. "I would love to."

"Great. I'll text you tomorrow and we can iron out the details." Logan attempted to hug her across the bar, but it came off as more of a pat on the back. Kelly was happy with any physical contact with Logan she could get.

Her intention hadn't been to spend the whole time with Logan, but she couldn't seem to tear herself away. There was just something about her that drew Kelly in, and Kelly wasn't sad about that. At all.

❖

Logan changed her shirt for the third time and looked at herself in the full-length mirror on the back of her closet door. This wasn't a date, so why was she so nervous? She wasn't the nervous type. It made no sense.

Satisfied with the way she looked, she closed the closet door, and headed into the living room. "I'll see you later," she said to Bear. "You've got fresh food and water, so I don't want to hear any complaints when I get back. I don't know how late I'll be. So don't wait up." She turned on the radio and the lamp on the end table, grabbed her keys, and headed out the door.

Kelly was waiting outside when she pulled up. Logan resisted the urge to jump out of the car and open the door for her. Not a date, she repeated in her head. "You look great," she said after Kelly slid onto the seat.

"No. I just—" She stopped, seemed to think about it and started again. "Thank you. I appreciate that. You do too."

Logan smiled matching Kelly's. "Good job not putting yourself down. You're learning."

"I'm trying."

"You're doing great. You are great. Believe it."

"Again," Kelly said. "Trying."

Logan rubbed Kelly's leg. She meant it as a friendly, comforting gesture, but it felt like so much more once she had done it.

"Umm, ready?"

"I am."

Logan took her hand off Kelly's leg and gripped the steering wheel. Maybe a little too tightly.

"You okay?" Kelly asked.

"Yes. Of course. Why?" Logan hoped she hadn't looked at Kelly too intensely or had some look go across her face.

"I don't know. You just—your knuckles are turning white on the steering wheel."

Logan loosened her grip. "Oh." She couldn't think of a reasonable excuse. "Didn't realize I was doing that."

"You sure you're okay?"

"I am. I should be asking you that." Logan pulled the car around onto the street. She glanced over at Kelly. "How are you doing?"

"I'm actually good. I miss having someone special in my life, but I don't think I miss Paula at all."

"That's great. I mean not about missing someone special. But about not missing Paula." Damn. That sounded awkward. She was usually much cooler than this. Or at least she pretended to be. What the hell? "So…"

"So…"

"So, did you have a good day at work? I mean walking dogs? I mean were all the dogs good for you today?" Again, not cool.

"I did have a good day. The dogs are always good for me. I keep treats in my pocket and they know they get them after their walk. So, they tend to behave. Dogs are always reliable that way. They don't lie or cheat. If they like you, they like you. They don't pretend."

Like Logan was doing? Pretending that she didn't like Kelly as much as she did? Was Kelly trying to tell her something? No. That didn't make sense.

"Do you know what I mean?"

Logan brought her thoughts back to the conversation. "I do. Animals are the best."

The conversation was light as Logan drove to the restaurant.

"Oh my God, look," Logan said, pointing at a notice on the bulletin board just inside the entrance.

"What?"

"They are having a trivia contest in the bar area tonight. What do you think? I think we should enter." She stepped closer to the notice. "First prize is a trip for two on the riverboat down the canal and a gift certificate for dinner."

"I don't know," Kelly said. "Trivia is just a hobby."

"It'll be fun. Come on. Let's do it."

"As long as you don't expect too much. I mean I'm not that—"

"Don't say it," Logan said. "Don't say you're not that smart. Don't put yourself down."

"Okay," Kelly said. "Let's give it a shot."

"Really?" Logan said. "Yes. You don't mind missing the movie?"

Kelly couldn't help but smile. Who knew a trivia contest could make someone so happy? Of course, just *being* with Logan made *her* happy. "I don't mind. If you don't mind losing."

"Stop. It's just for fun. Let's go sign up." Logan grabbed Kelly's hand and pulled her in the direction of the bar. Her hand felt so natural in Logan's.

"What can I get you?" the bartender asked.

"Well, Brian," Logan said, reading his name tag. "How do we go about signing up for the trivia contest?"

"Single or couple?" he asked.

"What?"

"Do you want to sign up as a couple..." He nodded in the direction of Kelly standing behind Logan. "Or do you want to sign up as a single player?"

Logan glanced over her shoulder at Kelly. "Couple. Definitely couple."

"Couples contest starts at nine. He pulled a clipboard from behind the bar and handed it to her with a pen. Put both your names down on the list. Be back by eight fifty. We'll be set up over in that area." He pointed to a group of tables by the back wall.

Kelly stood on her tiptoes and looked over Logan's shoulder at the list. There were eight other couples registered. Logan added their names.

They didn't have to wait long for their table or for their food once it was ordered.

"This is so good," Kelly said, twirling angel hair pasta onto her fork. "How is yours?"

"Equally as good. Good food. Good company. Thank you for agreeing to this."

Of course, Kelly wouldn't pass up an opportunity to spend time with Logan. "Thank you for inviting me."

They finished their meals and passed on dessert. "Don't want to be late for trivia," Logan explained. They fought briefly over paying the bill, each offering a credit card. Kelly finally relented and let Logan pay, insisting that it was her turn the next time they went out. And she certainly hoped there would be a next time.

They made their way over to the bar area where the tables were set up for the contest. Name tags were set at each seat. They found theirs and sat down. Logan peeled the backing off her name tag and pressed it to her shirt. She did the same with Kelly's. Kelly was hyper aware of how close to her breasts Logan's hand came when she placed the sticker on her shirt. She held her breath until Logan pulled her hand away. Her heart rate had picked up considerably.

"No pressure," Logan told her. "This is just for fun. Okay?"

"Yep. Fun. Got it. I'm picking up what you're putting down."

Logan laughed that laugh. "What?"

"Nothing. I was just trying to be cool and failing miserably."

"You didn't fail. I thought it was funny. You're so cute." A strange look crossed Logan's face. Almost like she regretted saying that.

Kelly wondered if she'd really meant it. She'd never thought of herself as cute and wondered if Logan really did.

It didn't take long for the tables surrounding them to fill up. Most of the other couples were boy-girl. The bartender, Brian, was playing MC for the evening. He explained the rules. One wrong answer took you out of the running.

"We got this," Logan said. She leaned in closer to Kelly and whispered in her ear. "As long as there isn't any sports trivia." She pulled back and chuckled.

"Any questions before we start?" Brian asked the small crowd. Several heads shook no. "We'll start with table one and move down the line in order. You'll have fifteen seconds to confer with your partner before answering."

Logan and Kelly were at table nine out of ten tables. Kelly figured they were in the order they'd signed up. No one had been eliminated by the time they got their second question.

"Who said you have to be odd to be number one? Was it Dr. Spock, Mr. Spock, Dr. Seuss, or Charlie Brown?"

Logan leaned so close that Kelly could feel heat radiating off her. Or maybe Kelly just got hot when Logan was so close. "I know it's not Mr. Spock," she said.

"It's Dr. Suess."

"Are you sure?"

"Positive. I've always loved that saying. Go ahead and answer."

Logan looked up at the MC. "Dr. Suess. Final answer."

He laughed. "No need to tell me it's your final answer. By the way, you are correct."

Logan pulled Kelly in for a hug. Kelly was really starting to like this game. The next couple failed to answer their question correctly. They were down to nine couples.

"How did you get so smart?" Logan whispered to Kelly. Her warm breath on her neck sent a shiver down Kelly's back.

"I'm not that smart. I just know a bunch of useless information. Too much time on my hands, I guess."

Logan pulled back and squinted at Kelly.

Kelly got the message. "Okay. I'm a genius. Happy now?"

"Yes. I am very happy that you are a genius." She smiled wide.

Stop smiling at me, Kelly thought. You don't know what it's doing to me. She felt the need to look away and put her attention on Brian who was asking the couple at table number four a question—which they missed.

Kelly was still trying to ignore Logan's body so close to her when their turn rolled around again.

"What is the plastic or metal coating at the end of your shoelace called? Is it a wamble, aglet, banlet, or tonguelet?"

"Oh shit," Logan whispered. "Any ideas?"

"It's not the last two," Kelly whispered back.

"So, a wamble or aglet?"

"I think a wamble is the rumbling sound your stomach makes."

"How in the world do you know that? Never mind. We've already established the fact that you're a genius. So, we're going with aglet?"

Kelly nodded, hoping to God she was right and at the same time hoping she was wrong to avoid another mind-numbing, body-tingling hug. Or maybe she desperately wanted another one. She was just so confused.

"Kelly? Aglet?"

"Yes."

"Brian, the answer is Aglet."

"You are correct. Nice job," Brian said.

Logan balled her fist and held it until Kelly fist-bumped her. No hug this time. Relief. Disappointment. More confusion.

Three rounds later, Kelly and Logan were still in the running along with two other couples. They were up again.

"Which Star Trek captain has an artificial heart? Was it Jean-Luc Picard, James Kirk, Kathryn Janeway, or Jonathan Archer?"

"This one's all yours," Kelly said.

"Easy one. Captain Jean-Luc Picard."

"Correct again. You two are on a roll."

It was Kelly's turn to decide how to celebrate the correct answer. A high five seemed like the safest choice.

After a couple more questions, it was down to Kelly and Logan and another couple. The other couple missed their question.

"If you get this question right," Brian said. "You'll win. But if you get it wrong, Sarah and Ben are still in it. Here we go. Who is the top scoring player in NBA history? LeBron James, Karl Malone, Magic Johnson, or Kareem Abdul-Jabbar?"

Logan and Kelly put their heads together. "Of course, it's a damn sports question," Logan said with a laugh. "I've never heard of Karl Malone, so I don't think it's him."

"I think that LeBron guy is newer than the other two, so let's eliminate him. What do you think?"

"No idea. Let's go with Kareem. That would be my guess. You okay with that?"

Kelly nodded. "Go for it. We have nothing to lose...except the whole game." She smiled.

"Oh, thanks. No pressure."

"We need your answer," Brian informed them.

"Kareem," Logan said, sounding less than confident.

"You are..." There was a long pause, more than likely for dramatic effect. "Correct."

Logan grabbed Kelly's face in her hands and kissed her. Hard. On the mouth. Kelly's stomach did a flip, and she was immediately wet. Holy shit.

Logan ended the kiss but still had Kelly's face in her hands. What the hell had she just done? She kissed Kelly and she liked it. A lot.

The shocked look on Kelly's face told Logan all she needed to know. She shouldn't have done that. Shit. Should she apologize? Pretend it didn't happen or didn't mean anything? Do what she really wanted to do—kiss Kelly again. No. That one was out of the question.

Apologize. That was the only thing to do. "Kelly, I'm so sor—"

"Hey, you two. Get a room. Come on stand up and take a bow. You're our winners. Let's give them a hand," Brian interrupted her.

Logan rose and held out her hand to Kelly, which she accepted and together they took a quick bow. Logan wasn't sure if the bright red blush creeping up Kelly's neck to her face was because of the kiss or the attention they were getting from everyone around them. Probably both.

Brian handed Logan a manila envelope with the words PRIZE PACKAGE handwritten on it. "Congratulations." He shook hands with each of them and turned his attention to chat with another couple.

Kelly looked like she hadn't quite recovered from the shock of that kiss. Logan struggled to find the words to explain and came up with none. The truth was she was very drawn to Kelly even though she knew she shouldn't be. Kelly had just had her heart broken and was in a very vulnerable place. Nothing could happen between them. Nothing. Logan was beginning to wish it could.

"Kelly?"

Kelly blinked a few times and turned to her.

"I'm sorry for the kiss. That wasn't…wasn't…I mean, I shouldn't have done that. I didn't mean it. I just felt…" She let the words trail off. Don't tell her what you felt, she thought. Don't add to the mistake.

Kelly shook her head. "No worries. I know it was just the heat of the moment and us winning."

Oh, but I did mean it. But I can't say that. Logan just nodded. "Right. But hey. We won. Thanks to you and your genius brain." She held up the manilla envelope.

"We did. We make a good team."

Logan was at a loss for what to do or say next. She rarely found herself in that position. Her body had calmed down from the stirrings caused by the ill-advised kiss. The kiss she longed to repeat but knew she couldn't. What the hell was happening to her? She had convinced herself that she didn't want a relationship. Didn't want to care about anyone in that way again, but here she was wanting Kelly. Was it more than lust for a woman she found so appealing? The feelings were too new for her to be able to figure it out. Yet. She needed to get a handle on this and not let it get out of control again.

"What are you thinking?" Kelly asked, shaking Logan out of her thoughts.

"Huh. Nothing major. Are you ready to go? Would you like to get a drink first?"

"I'm ready. I have wine at my apartment if you want to come up." She paused. "Oh wait. You said you don't drink. I'm assuming that includes wine."

Go up to Kelly's apartment? That might not be the wisest thing to do. "I would love to have a glass of wine at your apartment." What the hell, Logan? Why don't you listen to yourself? Bad idea. She pulled the keys from her pocket and shook them. "Shall we?"

They were quiet on the drive back to Kelly's. The argument in Logan's head was overwhelming. Go up with Kelly to her apartment? Make an excuse and go home? Keep things light and pretend you don't have a plethora of emotions swirling through you. You can do this. This is stupid. You kissed her and it could happen again if you aren't careful. I can control myself. I won't kiss her again. Okay. I'll buy this crap. Go ahead and go up with her. You can handle this.

She pulled into the parking lot convinced she could keep her emotions and her lips under control. She silently followed Kelly up the stairs to her apartment, making sure her eyes never roamed over Kelly's very cute rear end. Instead, she fixed them on each step that her foot landed on until they reached the top.

"So…" Kelly said.

"So…" Logan repeated.

"Wine? I have water or soda if that works better for you."

"I'll take a glass of wine. I don't usually drink, but I'm not a fanatic about it." Besides it might help me relax and stop this stupid dialogue going on in my head. Yeah. Good luck with that. I don't think anything is going to help. You keep going back and forth with the same garbage. You like Kelly. You shouldn't like Kelly. You don't want a relationship and suddenly you're thinking about the possibility of a relationship with her. The her who just broke up with her lying, cheating girlfriend and is in no condition to be hit on. Who said I was going to hit on her? What would you call that kiss if it wasn't hitting on her? It was just excitement over winning. Yeah. You keep telling yourself that. ENOUGH ALREADY. SHUT UP. Fine. You don't have to yell about it. Apparently, I do. Logan was convinced that she was going to drive herself crazy. She was still standing in the same spot when Kelly returned with two glasses of wine.

"Please," Kelly said. "Sit. Make yourself comfortable."

Logan sat on the couch. Kelly handed her a glass of wine and sat down next to her, leaving about a foot and a half of space between them. Logan was glad for the small distance.

"You seem like you're a million miles away," Kelly said.

"No. I'm here. Sorry."

"Why are you apologizing? You wouldn't let me get away with that."

Logan couldn't help but laugh. "True. I'm not sorry. But I am sorry for saying sorry."

It was Kelly's turn to laugh. "I don't accept your apology. No more sorrys."

"Okay. No more. Did you have a good time tonight?" Not counting the stupid kiss.

"I did. I can't believe we won." The smile that lit up her face went straight to Logan's heart.

"You did good. I can't believe you know the stuff you do. How did you learn all that?"

"It's mostly stuff I come across on the internet when I'm bored."

"You must be bored a lot."

"I know. I need to get a life."

Logan shook her head. "That's not what I meant."

"Well, it's true. Other than my job and occasionally getting together with Rachel and our other friend, Marley, I don't do much. I realized that I had spent so much of my time just waiting around for a little bit of attention from Paula. That was a major waste."

"I'm sorry."

"Oh my God. Did you just say the S word again?"

Logan put her hand over her mouth. "Oops. I did. Forget I said that. Go on."

Kelly sipped her wine, making eye contact with Logan over her glass. Logan held her gaze for several seconds before looking away. She took a sip of her own wine and remembered why she didn't drink. She didn't like the taste of alcohol. She was careful not to make a face. Logan felt so out of her element. Women didn't fluster her. She was the one who took control and set the rules. What was it about Kelly that was so different? She was real. She was a *what you see is what you get* kind of person. And Logan liked what she saw.

"There it is again," Kelly said.

"What?"

"That look on your face. Or maybe I should say the lack of a look on your face. You keep leaving the room. Where are you going?"

Think quick Logan. "I'm right here with you. I can't control if my face goes for a walk without me."

"Well, I like your face, so tell it to stay here with us."

"I'll do the best I can. Did you enjoy…" Logan stopped and realized she'd already asked that question. Get your head in the fucking game woman. Enough.

"Did I enjoy what?"

"Umm. Did you enjoy…umm…okay. Here is the truth. I was going to ask you if you enjoyed the evening then I realized that I already asked you that. I guess this wine is going to my head."

"One sip and your done for, huh?"

Logan held up her glass and looked at it. "Is that all I drank? Then I guess I can't blame it on the alcohol."

"I did enjoy the evening. And the company. And winning at trivia. Thank you for signing us up. I would have been too chicken to do it without you."

"Why? You're so good at it."

Kelly seemed to think about it for a few seconds. "I don't know. Being told you're worthless your whole childhood does something to you. It makes you believe you aren't good at anything."

"Do you still believe that?"

"I have my moments. But I have to tell you I am starting to hear your voice in the back of my head telling me not to put myself down."

"Oh wow. I'm not used to having people actually listen to me."

"I seriously doubt that."

"Why would you say that?"

"I'm sure you have women falling down at your feet, hanging on your every word. You seem like the kind of person that says jump and people…women…jump."

"I don't know whether to be flattered or insulted." Kelly had her attention now, which was much better than being lost in her revolving thoughts.

"Why would you be insulted?"

"I seem like the kind of person that would order people to jump?"

Kelly laughed and sipped her wine. "No. That's not what I mean. *If* you did. They would jump. Let me rephrase. Actually, let me think for a minute so I can say this right."

Logan was having a good time watching Kelly searching for the right words instead of the other way around.

"You have charisma. You draw people in. Don't tell me you don't know that. So, if you did tell…*ask* people, politely, to jump, they would be happy to do it for you."

Logan knew people—women seemed to like her. She never would have described herself as having charisma.

"You know it's true."

Logan wasn't sure how to answer that without sounding either like she was conceited or putting herself down.

"Nothing to say?"

"Nope. Yep. Thank you. I don't see myself that way but thank you."

"Maybe I'm not the only one that has been seeing themselves wrong. Should I take you into the bathroom to make you look at yourself in the mirror?"

"Touché. Okay. Jump."

"What?"

"I'm testing your theory. I'm asking you politely to jump. Please."

To Logan's surprise, Kelly put her nearly empty wine glass down, stood, jumped twice, and sat back down. "See. You say it. We women do it."

"Wow. What power I have. I hope I only use it for good and never for evil."

"I can't believe you would ever do anything evil."

Like kissing you without your permission less than a week after you broke up with your girlfriend. You can't imagine me doing anything evil like that?

"Do you not like the wine?"

Logan looked at her nearly full glass and scrunched up her face. "It was really the company I came for. I'm not much of a wine drinker."

"Why didn't you say something? I could have gotten you something else." Kelly stood, took the wine glass from Logan's hand, set it on the coffee table, and headed into the kitchen. She returned with a glass of soda and handed it to Logan.

"Thank you." Logan took a sip. Sprite. Much better. "I'm sorry I didn't mean to make you waste the wine." She realized she'd said sorry again and hoped Kelly didn't notice.

"Oh, it won't go to waste. I'll drink it. I doubt your germs will kill me."

"They might. You don't know where these lips have been." Logan regretted her words as soon as they were out of her mouth.

I do know where those lips have been, at least tonight, Kelly thought. The thought sent a surge of electricity through her. She didn't want to think about where they have been on other evenings. Logan had said that she didn't mean it. Kelly wished that wasn't true, but she had no choice but to believe her. "I'll use extra mouthwash tonight. Just to be safe," she joked. Humor had a way of defusing feelings. Especially feelings that she shouldn't be having.

"Good thinking."

Kelly suspected that Logan had been thrown by that kiss almost as much as she had been, but in an opposite way. Like in a regretful kind of way. That made Kelly sad. She finished her glass of wine and picked up Logan's. She held it up. "Here's to killing germs," she said.

"I'll drink to that," Logan added.

She didn't stay too much longer before she said good night. Her hug was not nearly as tight or as long as her hugs usually were. Kelly closed the door behind her and leaned against it. "What a night," she said out loud. "What a kiss." It hadn't been long, but it sure as hell was intense. At least it felt that way to Kelly. She wondered if Logan felt anything at all when she kissed her. Anything besides regret.

CHAPTER NINE

Logan pulled out the chair and sat across from her sister. The large house made Logan's apartment seem like a closet. Both Olivia and her husband, Daniel, had well-paying jobs and they had no trouble spending their money. Logan tried not to judge their extravagant lifestyle but silently worried that they might run into financial trouble if they weren't more careful.

"What's got you in a tizzy?" Olivia asked. Sometimes she sounded more like Logan's grandmother than her younger sister.

Logan ignored the urge to make fun of her for her choice of words. "I kissed Kelly."

"And that's a problem, why?" Olivia pushed a plate of cheese and crackers closer to Logan.

"She just broke up with her girlfriend."

"Again. What's the problem? She *broke up* with her girlfriend."

"It's the *just* part that's a problem. She hasn't even had time to heal, and I go and jump on her."

"You jumped on her too. That's a different story. Don't you need permission to do stuff like that nowadays. Like don't ask, don't tell? No that's not it. Getting consent and all that? Whatever it's called."

"I didn't actually jump on her."

"But you did kiss her?"

Logan was starting to regret even talking to Olivia about this. "Yes."

"Tongue?"

"Holy shit, Olivia. No. No tongue. But the point is I shouldn't have kissed her."

"Did she say that?"

"No. She didn't say anything. She just had this shocked look on her face."

"Did you talk to her about it at all?"

Logan grabbed a cracker from the plate and absently flipped it through her fingers. "I said I was sorry and that I didn't mean it."

"If someone kissed me and then said they didn't mean it I would be pissed." Olivia pointed to the cracker in Logan's hand. "Are you going to play with that or eat it?"

"Both," Logan said and popped it into her mouth.

"I wouldn't want someone kissing me unless they meant it," Olivia continued.

"I did mean it. I only said that because she looked like…I don't know…like I shouldn't have done it. Then to top it all off I acted like an ass later. My brain was sort of pinging all over the place and I had trouble keeping up with the conversation."

"None of this sounds good."

Logan shook her head. "That's what I'm trying to tell you. I don't know what to do about it."

"What are your options?"

"Talk to her about it or pretend like it never happened, I guess."

"And what do you want to do?"

Logan didn't have to think too hard to know the answer. "Kiss her again. But that's the wrong answer. I think the only way to play this is to pretend it didn't happen and just be her friend."

"Can you do that? I mean you want to kiss her, but you'll have to pretend you don't."

"Yes. I can do it. I'm not an animal, unable to control my urges."

"I think you've already proved that's not true."

"Yeah, well, it's not going to happen again."

"So just friends and leave it at that?"

Friends. She would hate to lose Kelly as a friend because of her stupid feelings. "Yes. Leave it at that," she repeated.

"Can I ask you a question?"

Logan knew that her sister would ask, no matter what her response was. She nodded.

"I thought you didn't want a relationship and all of a sudden you are gaga over this girl. What gives?"

"I don't think *gaga* is the right word. And I'm not saying I want a relationship." She thought about it for a couple of seconds. "Then again, I'm not saying I don't. I don't know. Can you tell this one is confusing the hell out of me?"

"I can. I'm not sure I've ever seen you like this. You are usually so sure of yourself and what you want."

"I know." She bit her bottom lip. "I don't like this. This feeling of not being in total control."

"What if you don't see her for a while? Let your feelings calm down."

The thought of that sent a wave of panic through Logan. Not see her? No. That wouldn't work. For one thing she promised Kelly that she could see Bear any time she wanted and for another she didn't *want* to stop seeing her. That would be like punishing herself for being attracted to her. "Yeah. No. Don't want to do that. Just gonna pretend like everything is copacetic. No problems here." She held her arms out to the side. "No crushes or feelings or going gaga here."

"If you say so," Olivia said.

"I do. It's my only option." At least for now.

❖

"Thanks for letting me come over," Kelly said. "I'm supposed to meet Rachel down at the bar in an hour. It's earlier than we normally get together, but she can't stay long. I thought I would sneak in a visit with Bear first."

"Of course. Anytime," Logan responded. "Come on in. He's in the bedroom, I think. I'll go get him. Sit. Be comfortable." She disappeared down the hallway and reappeared with Bear in her arms. "Here he is."

Kelly sat on the couch and Logan placed Bear on her lap. She kissed the top of his head. It had been a couple of weeks since she'd seen him last, and she really did miss him.

"You haven't been around in a while. Everything okay?"

Kelly had avoided Logan and by proxy Bear, on purpose. That kiss Logan hit her with had thrown her much more than she had initially realized. Which was just plain stupid. No, she wasn't calling herself stupid. She looked up at Logan as if Logan could read her mind and she had to reassure her she wasn't putting herself down. Getting so worked up by a kiss that meant nothing to the other person and lasted only a few seconds was stupid.

"What?" Logan asked.

"What what?"

"I don't know. You had a strange look on your face."

"Did I?" She stopped herself before she added *sorry*. "Didn't mean to. How have you and Bear been? Sorry I haven't been around. I picked up another client." That was true. She didn't bother mentioning that it didn't really make her day any longer and replaced a client that had recently moved.

"I understand. Sometimes business gets in the way of life. Just make sure you don't let business take *over* your life. How are you doing with everything else?"

Was Logan talking about the two of them? Or the kiss?

"With the breakup, I mean?"

"Oh. Yeah. I'm doing good. I thought I would miss Paula, but I really don't. It wasn't like she was a part of my daily life. It was more like someone who would pop in on occasion and pop out again just as fast. And now that I know the truth about her, I find I'm more angry than anything else."

"I get that."

"I know I have got to let that go at some point. It doesn't hurt her to hold this resentment. It makes my guts feel like they're tied up in knots. It's not a good feeling."

"I am living proof that the feeling will go away. Not overnight. But it will."

"I appreciate that. In fact, I appreciate your support throughout this whole thing." Without Logan's insight and help she might not have broken up with Paula and in the process found out the truth.

"Of course. Oh geez. What kind of a hostess am I? I haven't even offered you anything to drink. Or maybe something to munch on?" Logan said.

Kelly laughed. "I noticed you were failing your hostess duties but didn't want to mention it."

"Stop. You're making fun of me now."

"I am. And I don't need anything to eat or drink. You can make me a drink in a little while when you go on duty and I'm at the bar with Rachel."

"Sloe gin fizz. You got it. So, this is a gin and Bear it kind of day."

"You've been waiting a long time to pull that out again. Haven't you?"

"I have. Thanks for giving me the opportunity."

"What if I want to mix it up and have…oh, I don't know… maybe sex on the beach."

"Ooh. You want to try to have sex on the beach?"

Kelly's stomach did a flip-flop at the thought. She swallowed hard before answering. "It could be interesting. As long as sand didn't get into places sand shouldn't be." She gave a nervous laugh.

"Good point."

Kelly had the urge to flirt—if that's what they were even doing—more. "How about you? Sex on the beach?"

"Not the drink. But sex on an actual beach could be fun. Know any beaches close by? I'll drive." She winked.

Yes. Definitely flirting.

Kelly was a bit flustered. She wasn't used to someone flirting with her, let alone someone so out of her league as Logan was. "Can we be back in time for me to meet Rachel?" Lame.

"Oh, baby, we wouldn't be back for the rest of the night."

Against her will, she felt a rush of wetness, and it took all her willpower to resist squirming against it. Her turn to respond. It was hard to think with the rush of blood leaving her extremities and brain and settling squarely in her center. She struggled to come up with a response.

Logan watched as Kelly's face turned a deep shade of red. She was sure she'd overstepped with the flirting. The woman just broke up with her girlfriend, she reminded herself. Way too soon for this, even if it was just in fun. The problem was, Logan wanted it to be more than just fun. As much as she tried fighting it, her heart wasn't listening to her arguments. Might be time to change the subject.

"Let me just text Rachel and tell her I'll be indisposed for the rest of the evening," Kelly said, surprising Logan.

She was more than willing to continue playing this game if Kelly was. "Oh, what the hell. Tell her you'll be busy for the next week."

"You think you can keep me entertained for a whole week?"

Wow. She had no idea Kelly had this in her. "Honey, I can *entertain* you until you're begging me to stop. A whole week would just be the beginning."

"That would be a first," Kelly said, seeming to turn more serious.

"What would?"

Kelly cleared her throat and took so long to answer that Logan thought she wasn't going to. "Having someone *entertain* me." She used air quotes.

"What do you mean?"

Kelly stared up at the ceiling for several long beats before answering. "No one I've ever been with has cared much about whether I had a good time or not. A lot of it…most of it…maybe all of it…has been pretty much one-sided."

"Are you kidding me? That's just wrong." One more reason for Kelly to have low self-esteem. She'd obviously only been with assholes.

"Paula said it was my fault that I never…" She let the words drift off.

"You never had an orgasm?"

Kelly nodded.

"With anyone?"

"I can't believe I'm saying this, but only by myself."

"That just pisses me off and makes me want to hunt down your exes and punch them in the face."

Kelly laughed. "No one was ever willing to commit a crime for me before."

"I wouldn't consider it a crime as much as justice served."

"I appreciate that."

"I expect a full list of your exes and their addresses. You may want to start saving your pennies for my bail money."

"It's the least I could do."

"I'm flattered that you would do the least you could do for me, when I'm willing to go to prison for you."

Kelly laughed. Logan loved the sound of it. She vowed to make Kelly laugh every chance she got.

"Might be best not to track anyone down to beat them."

"You think losing you is punishment enough?"

"Hmm. Wasn't thinking that, but we can go with that if you want."

"They probably have no idea what they missed out on. Because they are complete idiots."

"Maybe I was the idiot for putting up with it."

"You're putting yourself down again."

"The truth is I was an idiot. I'm hoping I learned enough from my past mistakes to never let that happen again." She ran her hand down Bear's back and was rewarded with a loud purr.

"We all make mistakes. I sure as hell have made my share."

"I find that hard to believe. You seem so put together," Kelly said.

"Ahh. Looks can be deceiving."

Kelly's phone pinged before she had a chance to answer. She pulled it from her pocket and looked at the text that had just come through. "Oh man, Rachel is downstairs waiting for me. The last hour just flew by."

"Does this mean the beach is out?"

"Damn. Next time. I don't want Rachel to get mad at me."

"Understood. My shift starts in an hour. I guess I'll see you down there. I'll have to settle for making you a drink instead of taking you for a ride."

Kelly smiled. She gently shifted Bear off her lap and set him on the couch next to her. He immediately reached a paw out and laid it on her leg. She scooted out from under it.

Logan gave her a tight hug at the door. "See you soon," she said.

She settled herself down on the couch next to Bear. "Well, that was interesting," she said to him. "Kelly sure has had some hard knocks. She deserves so much more than the crap and the people she's had to deal with."

❖

Kelly spotted Rachel in her usual seat as soon as she walked into the bar.

"Hey. Sorry I'm late. I lost track of time. I was visiting Bear."

"And Logan?"

"She lives there, so yeah. She's hard to ignore. I like her, Rachel. I mean, really like her."

"I'm not surprised. I know I keep saying how hot she is, but she really does seem nice too."

"She is."

"What can I get you?" the young bartender asked Kelly. Helen, her name tag said. It was unusual for Kelly and Rachel to be there before Logan's shift.

"Just a glass of water for now," Kelly said.

"You aren't going to get a drink?" Rachel asked her. Rachel's was already a quarter of the way gone.

"I will. But not just yet."

"Waiting for Logan?" Rachel asked once Helen was out of hearing range.

"Yeah. Something like that."

"Exactly like that. What's going on between the two of you?"

"Nothing. Friendship." She turned toward Rachel. "I wish it was more. But I know it will never be, so I…I don't know. I just want to be around her."

"And Paula?"

Just hearing her name made Kelly's stomach drop. Not out of a sense of missing her or wishing they were still together. It was more out of leftover resentment. "Paula is out of my life and never should have happened. You were so right about her and I'm sorry I didn't listen to you."

"I'm just glad you're out of that mess now." Rachel sipped her drink. "Why do you say it can never be more than friendship with Logan?"

"She and I are in different worlds. She is so far out of my league."

"That's not true."

"What are you talking about? You've seen her and to use your own words, she's hot."

"And?"

"And I'm not. Okay, I'm not ugly. You guys have pounded that into my head enough that I'm starting to believe you. But Logan could have anybody. Why would she want me?"

"Because you're great. You're kind, caring, and beautiful, inside and out. Anyone would be lucky to have you."

"I don't think Logan is looking for a relationship anyway. She's had some hurt in her life," Kelly said. She didn't feel right giving Rachel the few details she knew about Logan's past.

"Did she tell you that?"

"More or less."

"And you're sure you aren't making assumptions that aren't there?"

"Yeah. I'm sure. She's not into relationships. I think one-night stands are more her speed. But that doesn't stop me from liking her."

"So, what are you going to do?"

"Nothing. Just keep being her friend. What else can I do? I'll just enjoy the time I do get to spend with her."

Kelly was surprised to see Logan coming in through the back of the bar area, dressed in her work clothes, minus the apron around her waist. She was at least forty minutes early for her shift.

"Hey," Kelly said as she approached them. "How come you're here so early?"

"It was lonely upstairs without you. I hope you don't mind that I came down to join you." A smile lit up her face and Kelly's heart melted.

"Of course not," Kelly said.

"Should we grab a table instead of sitting at the bar?" Rachel asked.

Kelly silently mouthed *thank you.*

"Hey, great. I would appreciate that. Let me just grab a soda and…" She lifted Kelly's glass and sniffed it. "Water?"

Kelly nodded.

"Let me get you a drink. Rachel, need a refill?"

Rachel held up her glass. "I'm good."

Logan set about getting them drinks while Kelly and Rachel made their way to a table. There were plenty to choose from as it was still early. Rachel sat across from Kelly, leaving a chair on either side of her empty.

It didn't take long for Logan to join them. She set a drink in front of Kelly. It wasn't her usual sloe gin fizz. She tentatively took a sip. It was good. Very good.

"Sex on the beach," Logan said.

Kelly smiled and took a larger sip.

Rachel looked from one to the other with a confused look on her face.

"Long story," Kelly said. "I thought I would try something different, and Logan was kind enough to remember."

"How could I forget?" Logan said and winked at Kelly.

Kelly's stomach clenched at the memory of their recent, flirty conversation.

"Do you like it?" Logan asked.

"I do. I may have a new regular. You're going to have to ask me if I'm here to have sex on the beach and Bear." She laughed at herself. "Which makes no sense."

Logan joined in the laughter.

"Would you like to taste it?" Kelly asked Rachel, not wanting her to feel left out.

She shook her head. "No. That's okay. I've had them before." She turned her attention to Logan. "How is it working out with Bear?"

"He's great. I'm so grateful to Kelly for bringing him into my life. And then by the same token you could say that Bear brought Kelly into my life. For which I am equally as grateful."

"Yes," Rachel said. "She's the best." She held up her drink. "To Kelly."

Kelly hoped Rachel would leave it at that and didn't start listing all her qualities to try to get Logan interested in her.

"I'll drink to that," Logan said and took a drink of her soda.

Kelly gave Rachel a sideways glance hoping she got the message to stop.

"How's your mom doing, Logan?" Kelly asked, changing the subject.

"She's good. She's met Bear through Facetime and thinks he's adorable. The arthritis in her knees makes it hard to climb the stairs to my apartment."

"That's too bad that she can't visit," Rachel said.

Kelly continued to sip her drink, watching Rachel and Logan interact over the rim of her glass. Before she knew it, her glass was empty.

"You must have really liked that," Logan said. Before she had a chance to object, Logan was up getting her a refill.

"Can I get you another too?" she asked Rachel when she returned with Kelly's drink.

"Sure." Rachel handed Logan her empty glass. Helen has my credit card. Just put both our drinks on my tab."

"No problem. I've got this," Logan said.

"You don't have to do that," Kelly said. "It was Rachel's turn to pay anyway."

"Rachel can pay next time. Today, they are on the house."

"Thank you," Rachel said. "I appreciate it."

"Me too," Kelly said.

"I can see why you like her so much," Rachel whispered when Logan was far enough away.

"Right? She's the best. I wish I stood a chance." Kelly watched Logan as she made the drink. "Shh. She's coming back."

Logan set the drink in front of Rachel.

"Thank you."

"I should probably go and get ready for my shift," Logan said. "I'm glad I got a chance to get to know you a little better," she said to Rachel.

"Ditto."

"See ya," Logan said, as she rubbed Kelly's shoulder. The small gesture sent a surge through Kelly. Any contact from Logan seemed to do that to her. Logan disappeared into the back room behind the bar.

Kelly realized Rachel was watching her as she was watching Logan. "What?"

"I think she likes you."

"I hope she likes me."

"No. I think she really likes you."

"You're wrong. She's just nice to everyone. She got you another drink too."

"She didn't touch my shoulder when she left."

It still felt warm where Logan had put her hand on Kelly. "She just knows me better."

"Okay. You keep telling yourself that."

Kelly decided a change of subject was in order. "How is Mark doing?"

"He's good. Up for a promotion at work. That's why I can't stay long. We are going to get together at his boss's house. He thinks he needs to do some sucking up."

"And you wanted to come out drinking first?"

"Of course. I needed to be lubricated before plastering a smile on my face and pretending I was happy to be there. I figure if I have two drinks here and three drinks there, no one will know I have four drinks in me."

"That would make five."

Rachel put her finger to her lips. "Shh. Mark thinks four is my limit."

"I'll never tell."

"Good.

They kept the conversation light for the next thirty minutes until Rachel took her leave. Kelly didn't feel like going home to an empty apartment, so she made her way to the bar and slid onto a stool on the end. She was lucky to find an empty seat.

"Well, hello there," Logan said.

"Hi. Long time, no see."

"I know. It's been the longest forty minutes of my life," Logan said with a smile.

"You know how to make a girl feel good. Another drink might make me feel even better." Kelly held up her glass.

Logan put her hand to her chest. "What?" She feigned surprise. "You're going over your two-drink limit."

"I am living dangerously these days."

"I hope it's not too dangerous."

"I'm tired of taking a walk on the *mild* side."

Logan burst out laughing. "Time for the *wild* side instead?"

"Something like that. If we can count three drinks as being wild."

"For you? Yep. That's wild."

Kelly insisted on paying for the drink and pushed her credit card at Logan until she relented. She was in an unusual mood. She'd spent time with Bear, with Rachel, and best of all, with Logan. Another drink was called for.

She sat at the bar, nursing her sex on the beach, and watched Logan make drinks and interact with the customers. She was fascinated at how smoothly she did it all. Kelly finished her third drink before she knew it and asked for another.

"You sure you can handle it?" Logan asked her.

"I'm a big girl. I can get an Uber if I need to."

"You can crash at my place if you want," Logan said.

The thought was very appealing to Kelly. She downed her fourth drink without much trouble, and it was the other evening bartender, Joe, who made her another while Logan was off to the bathroom or somewhere.

Kelly lost track of how many drinks she had. She did know that the bar was starting to slant to the left, although a couple of times it took a sharp turn to the right. She vaguely remembered Logan helping her up the stairs.

Logan was surprised that Kelly had had enough drinks to get so drunk. Not that she didn't have every right to break loose after the week she'd had. Once she had her safely up the stairs she walked her to the bedroom, helped her remove her pants and sat her on the bed while she rustled through her drawer to get a long T-shirt. "Can you take off your shirt and put this on?" Logan asked her.

"Of course. I can get dressed like a big girl." Kelly giggled.

"I'm going to go get you some water. I'll be right back." Logan left the room to give Kelly some privacy. She returned with the water to find Kelly flat on her back in the bed, under the covers.

The T-shirt, along with Kelly's shirt and bra, were thrown on the foot of the bed. "Oh. Forgot my undies," she said and appeared to be wiggling out of them. They joined the rest of the pile of clothes.

"Okay then," Logan said. "As long as you're comfortable." She put the glass of water on the nightstand.

"I'm comfta—ta—bul." She put her arms out. "Come here. I need a hug." It was more of a whiny command than a request.

Logan pulled the covers higher up on Kelly before leaning down and hugging her. She brushed the hair out of her face and kissed her on the forehead. "Get some sleep, sweetie." Logan grabbed her toothbrush from the bathroom and her nightshirt and robe from the hook on the back of the door, backed out of the room, and shut off the light. She left the door cracked open in case Kelly needed her. She changed her clothes and brushed her teeth in the second bathroom, before settling down on the couch. She turned the TV on and lowered the volume until it was barely audible. It was quite a while before she fell into a fitful sleep. It wasn't that the couch was uncomfortable. It was that the person she was so attracted to was asleep in the other room—in her bed.

She got up much earlier than she usually did when she worked late. She slipped on her bathrobe and peeked into the bedroom. Kelly was still fast asleep. The blankets were askew, and Logan wondered if Kelly's sleep had been as restless as her own had been.

She made her way to the kitchen and started a pot of coffee. She considered making breakfast but wasn't sure if she should wake Kelly up to eat. Probably better to let her sleep. She probably needed it.

Sunlight was streaming through the window when Kelly opened her eyes—blinding light, painful light. She didn't know where she was but thought maybe it was hell with how hard her head was pounding. And what had crawled into her mouth and died?

She opened one eye a slit and looked around. She recognized the figures on the dresser. She was in Logan's bedroom. And oh shit! She was naked. She had no memory of even going to Logan's apartment. And how come she had no clothes on? What had they done that she didn't remember? Was she one of Logan's one-night stands? The bed looked like they had done more than sleep. What the hell had happened? Too many questions without any answers.

She found her clothes in a heap on the floor by the foot of the bed and quickly slipped them on—well, as quickly as her pounding head let her. In the bathroom she used the toilet and rinsed her mouth out with water. It didn't help. She tried to finger comb her hair without much success.

She sheepishly tiptoed out of the room and found Logan in the kitchen pouring a cup of coffee. The smell of it almost made Kelly vomit. She considered slipping out the door without saying anything but didn't get a chance.

Logan turned around. The bathrobe she was wearing opened, and Kelly could see she had a nightshirt on. "Hey there. How are you feeling? You had quite a night last night."

Quite a night? Quite a night with Logan? "Not so good. I think I'm going to go home."

"I made coffee. You don't need to rush off. I can make breakfast."

Just the thought of it made Kelly's stomach flip. "No. I... what time is it? I have to walk a dog at eleven."

"It's early. A little after seven. I'm surprised to see you up so early after last night."

Kelly wanted to know what had happened and at the same time was afraid to find out. They had been flirting in Logan's apartment before Kelly went down to meet Rachel in the bar. Had Logan taken it seriously and taken advantage of her in her intoxicated state? Kelly might have been a willing participant considering her growing feelings for Logan. But the last thing she wanted to be was another notch on Logan's bedpost.

"Kelly, why don't you sit down? You're looking a little pale. I don't think you should be driving right now."

"I'm fine." Just confused.

"Seriously. Sit. If you don't want coffee at least drink some water." She poured a glass from a pitcher in the refrigerator and led Kelly to the couch.

Kelly had no choice but to sit and drink it.

"Do you need some Advil?"

"Yes. Please." Anything to stop the pounding in her head. Maybe it would help her think clearly and figure out some things. She was sure something had happened between them. Why else would she have woken up naked in Logan's bed?

Logan disappeared down the hall and returned with medicine in hand. "I'd be happy to take you to your client's if you don't feel up to driving."

A wave of nausea overtook her when she shook her head. "I'll be okay. I just need a few minutes." She didn't know if she was trying to convince Logan or herself. It took several sips of water to get the pills all the way down. Damn. Why hadn't she stuck to her two-drink rule? She'd seen her mother hung over more times than she could count. How could anyone get drunk again after feeling this awful?

"Can I get you anything? Coffee? Something to eat?" Logan asked.

"No. There's no way I can eat. I may never eat again. I know I'll never drink again."

Logan laughed and then covered her mouth. "Sorry. You'll be fine and forget all about this."

She apparently already forgot most of it.

"Do you want to go back to bed for a while?"

"No." She was confused. Logan was trying to get her back to bed? As sick as she felt she couldn't believe Logan expected that. She wasn't sure if she should feel flattered or pissed off. She was leaning toward the latter. She just wanted to go home. What the hell had happened between them?

CHAPTER TEN

"Thanks for meeting me early," Kelly said to Rachel. "I wanted to talk to you without Marley around." They found an empty table in the food court and sat down across from each other.

"What's up?"

"I think I slept with Logan."

Rachel sat up straighter. "What? Wait. What do you mean you *think* you slept with her? How can you not know?"

"Remember the other night when we were at the bar, and you left early?"

"Of course."

"I stayed later."

"Yeah." She made a rolling motion with her hand, indicating she wanted Kelly to get to the point.

"I had too much to drink," Kelly said.

"You never drink too much."

"It was the first time. I got drunk. Very drunk. I woke up the next morning in Logan's bed. Naked."

"Was she naked too?"

"She was already up when I woke up. She had a bathrobe on with a nightshirt under it and no pants."

"Like she'd gotten up and just threw something on?" Rachel rubbed her chin.

"That's what I thought too. The bed was a mess. Like there had been quite the wrestling match."

"Holy cow. And you don't remember it?"

"No."

"You slept with Logan and have no memory of it? That's wild."

"Rachel, you aren't helping here."

"Oh geez. I'm sorry. But I told you she was into you. What happened in the morning? I mean did she say anything about it?"

"She said she was surprised to see me up so early after last night. She also asked me if I wanted to go back to bed."

"Like do it again? Have sex again?"

"I'm not sure. I don't know what to think."

"What did you do?"

Kelly leaned in. The food court was starting to fill up around them. "Nothing. I waited until I felt good enough to drive and went home. It's not like I could ask her if we had been intimate," she whispered.

"How would you have ended up naked in her bed if you weren't?"

"No idea. I could have died from embarrassment."

"Have you heard from her since then?"

"She called twice. I didn't answer."

"And you didn't call her back?"

"Call who back?" Marley asked as she approached the table.

Rachel looked from Marley to Kelly and raised her eyebrows.

"Logan," Kelly answered.

"That's the hot bartender. Right?"

Kelly cringed at the description that she and Rachel used to use.

"Yes," Rachel answered. "You're here early."

"We're doing inventory today and got our lunch breaks sooner than normal. I didn't know you were here already. I've just been wandering the mall. I've only got a half hour left. I'm going to grab something to eat."

"You go ahead," Rachel said. "We'll get something in a minute."

"You guys all right? Kelly looks like she's ready to crawl out of her skin."

"We're fine. Just talking. Nothing major," Rachel said.

"Okay. If you don't want me to hear, I'll be over there getting Chinese. Want to signal me when it's safe to come back?"

"Don't be silly," Kelly said. "Come back as soon as you get your food."

"We'll continue this as soon as she goes back to work," Rachel said as soon as Marley was out of earshot. "Let's go get our food."

Marley returned to the table with a paper plate piled high with lo mein, fried rice, and cashew chicken. Rachel had half a sub and a bowl of soup. Kelly had a small salad.

"That's all you're eating?" Marley asked her.

She hadn't had much of an appetite since the night she got drunk. "Not very hungry."

"But you're always hungry. You sure you're all right?"

"I'm fine."

"She's fine," Rachel chipped in.

Marley looked from one to the other. "Ooookaaay," she said, dragging out the word.

Rachel seemed to make sure their conversation was superficial, sticking to light topics and questions. Kelly was grateful.

"So, Logan called you and you didn't call her back?" Rachel asked, picking up their conversation as soon as Marley went back to work.

"Yeah. I'm scared to talk to her. I don't know if it meant anything to her or if it was just one of her one-night stands. I mean she said the kiss meant nothing. Why would sex be anything different?"

"Are you going to avoid her forever? And Bear?"

Bear? She hadn't even thought about him in all this. She couldn't stand the thought of never seeing him again. Or Logan for that matter. She needed to put this out of her mind. Pretend like it never happened and try to maintain a friendship with her. She was sure Logan would want to do that much. Stay friends. Otherwise, Kelly doubted she would have bothered calling. "No, I—" Kelly started to explain when her phone pinged with an incoming text. "It's from Logan," she told Rachel.

"What does it say?"

Kelly read it out loud. "Hey there. Are you okay? Haven't heard from you in a while."

"You should answer it. She obviously cares about you."

❖

It had been a week since Logan had heard from Kelly. She'd called and left several messages, but Kelly hadn't gotten back to her. She didn't know if Kelly was somehow mad at her or if she was embarrassed for getting drunk. Either way she wanted to find out what was going on. She decided that if Kelly didn't answer her text she was going to drive to her house and make sure she was all right.

She threw her phone on the bed, stretched out next to Bear, and ran a hand down his back. "I don't know what the heck is up with your Mama Kelly. But I'm starting to get worried about her."

He blinked a couple of times at her but had no answers.

She grabbed her phone as soon as it pinged. It was a text from Kelly. "Finally," she said.

I'm fine. Lunch with Marley and Rachel.

"That's not as reassuring as I'd hoped it would be. I still don't know what is going on with her." She looked over at the cat. "You got no advice for me here, big guy? Come on. You used to live with her. No idea why she suddenly disappeared?"

He licked his paw in response.

"Me either." Damn. Why did she feel so restless lately? She got up, grabbed her keys, and drove to her mother's house. There was always something that needed to be done there and doing it would help keep her mind off Kelly.

"Hi, honey," her mother said. "I wasn't expecting you today. Everything all right?"

"Can't a daughter visit her mother and see if she needs anything done?" She sat on the glider swing next to her mother. It was a beautiful day to be sitting outside on the front porch.

"You can. You just usually don't. I have iced tea in the fridge if you want some. You can fetch me a refill while you're in there." Her mother handed Logan her nearly empty glass with a smile. "Please and thank you."

Logan took the glass and headed inside. She grabbed a piece of American cheese from the refrigerator after replacing the pitcher of tea. With a glass in each hand and the cheese perched between her lips, she joined her mother once again on the porch.

"What's going on with you?" her mother asked after ten minutes of silence.

Logan shook her head. She wasn't sure how to explain her feelings when she didn't totally understand them herself. "I'm not sure. You remember I told you I got Bear from a woman named Kelly?"

Her mother nodded.

"She's visited him several times and we've gotten together as well. We even won a trivia contest." She paused thinking back to that night and the kiss that almost sent Kelly running. She wondered if that kiss had anything to do with the way Kelly was obviously avoiding her now. Probably not. She'd seen Kelly since then and Kelly seemed fine.

"So, what's the problem?"

"I thought we were friends, but she seems to have ghosted me."

"Ghosted you? What does that mean?" her mother asked.

"She's not answering or returning my phone calls and the one text that she did answer was vague. I don't know if I did something to offend her."

"What could you have done?"

Logan sipped her iced tea while she thought about it. Other than the kiss, she had no idea. "I don't know."

"How do you know she isn't just busy?"

"I guess I don't." She pushed off the porch floor, causing the glider to gently sway. "It just seems strange and out of character for her."

"Have you asked her about it?"

"I would if she would talk to me. Do you think showing up at her door would be a bad idea?"

"The fact that you even asked me that question tells me that *you* think it's a bad idea."

Logan nodded. If there was one thing she could count on it was good advice from her mother. "Yeah. But I don't know what else to do."

"Are you sure she's just a friend?"

"What do you mean?"

"It's not unusual for friendships to have gaps. I know you've experienced that before with other friends. But you seem more worked up over this than you normally would be."

Logan was silent while she rolled the question around in her head. Yes, she was attracted to Kelly. Yes, she would have liked to explore the possibilities of more with her if the timing was right. Yes, she was worried that Kelly would retreat from her life with no explanation. "I care about her." That much was true.

"And you didn't care about your other friends? Or maybe you didn't care about them in the same way?"

"I guess I'm trying to figure that out."

"Honey, I know Judith hurt you. But not all women are like her. You've had a shield around your heart since you found out she cheated on you. It might be time to let that go and let someone else in to love you."

Logan couldn't argue with that. "How do I do that if Kelly won't talk to me?"

"Give her time. You can't make someone else love you, but if you are willing to show her your true self and be honest with her, you might stand a chance. If it's meant to be, she'll be back around. Maybe she's trying to figure out her own feelings."

Logan hadn't considered that. The thought was as much anxiety provoking as it was comforting. If Kelly had pulled back to examine her own feelings, there was a good chance that she would conclude that the possibly of a relationship with Logan was something she wasn't interested in. If that was the case, there was nothing Logan could do about it. And that thought scared her.

❖

As hard as Logan tried to keep Kelly out of her head, she kept sneaking in. It was another four days before she heard from her again.

The text was brief. *Sorry I've been MIA. A lot going on.*

Logan took several long seconds trying to formulate her response. *No worries. I just miss you.*

After a few minutes staring at her phone awaiting a response that didn't come, Logan set it on the coffee table and went to make lunch. Relax, her sister had told her. Give her time was her mother's advice. Both, hard to do.

She'd just finished chopping eggs for an egg salad sandwich when another text came through. She tried to ignore it and finish the task at hand, but anxiety got the best of her, and she abandoned the eggs to retrieve her phone and read the text.

She let out a grunt when she realized it was from her sister. *How are you doing? How's it going with Kelly? Anything new there?*

Logan: *Want to come over for lunch? Egg salad sandwiches and tomato soup.*

Olivia: *What kind of an answer is that?*

Logan: *It's the NO ANSWER answer. I'll fill you in if you come over.*

Olivia: *That's blackmail.*

Logan: *No. It's a bribe. See you in fifteen.*

Logan set about finishing lunch and setting the table for two. It took her sister sixteen minutes to arrive.

"You're late," Logan told her.

"You're lucky I'm here at all. I was catching up on *General Hospital*. Sundays are my only days to do that."

"How are Luke and Laura these days?" Logan poured them each a glass of soda.

"Wow. You are way out of the loop. That was so nineteen eighties. Laura is married to someone else, and Luke is dead, for like the eleventh time."

"Which means he's not really dead?"

"Is anyone ever really dead on a soap opera? Speaking of soap operas, I'm here. Spill. Tell me what's going on with Kelly." Olivia pulled out a chair and sat.

Logan sat across from her, unfolded her napkin, and placed it across her lap. "Nothing. There is nothing going on with Kelly."

"What? You got me here under false pretenses."

"No, I didn't. I'm filling you in." She took a bite of her sandwich, chewing slowly.

"You haven't heard from her?"

"As a matter of fact, she texted me a little while ago," Logan said. "Didn't say much." She read Kelly's text and her response out loud. "And then crickets again. No answer."

"I'm sorry."

"It's funny. I mean not funny ha ha, but funny strange. I finally decide that someone is worth giving my heart to and she disappears on me."

"What happened to you worrying about it being too soon for her? Maybe that's the case. Maybe she's figuring things out."

"She's given me the impression, when she was talking to me, that she didn't miss Paula and was glad she was out of that mess."

Olivia dipped the corner of her sandwich into her soup and watched it drip before taking a bite. Why anyone would want to eat a soggy sandwich was something Logan would never understand. "Thoughts?" Logan asked.

"I'm not sure."

"That's helpful."

Logan's phone pinged and her heart dropped to her stomach. She had protected herself for so long after Judith's betrayal. It made her mad how much her current emotions seemed to be at the beck and call of Kelly.

"Is that from her?" Olivia asked.

Logan turned her phone over. It was. Logan nodded.

"What does it say?"

"Can we get together?"

"Well, there you go. Answer her. Wait. Don't answer yet. Let it sit for a while. Don't seem too eager."

"Olivia, I'm not into playing games."

"It's not a game. Let her wonder for a bit what your answer is going to be. It only works in your favor to keep her waiting."

"And that's not a game?"

"No. It's a smart move. Put your phone down and finish your lunch."

Logan reluctantly did as she was told, although her appetite seemed to have abandoned her.

After her last spoonful of soup Logan picked up her phone. She avoided eye contact with Olivia as she typed out her response to Kelly's text. *Yes. I would like that. We still have the tickets for the trip on the Riverboat down the canal. Would you like to do that?*

She set her phone down again and folded her hands.

"Praying?"

Logan laughed. "No, although maybe that's not a bad idea." She closed her eyes. "Dear God, Universe, Supreme Being. Please..." She opened her eyes. "I don't know what I am supposed to pray for. It seems wrong to ask that Kelly like me. I mean I want her to like me because she does. Not because God makes her do it."

Olivia laughed so hard she snorted. "I don't think that's how God works."

"What should I ask for?"

"Been a while since you've prayed."

"I'm ashamed to say yes."

"Ask that whatever is supposed to happen happens and that you are able to accept whatever that may be."

Logan looked up. "What she said."

As if it was an answer to her prayer, Kelly's text came through. *That would be good. When?*

Logan used her phone to look up the times available for the Riverboat ride. *Does today at five work for you?*

Sure. Kelly answered.

Should I pick you up about four thirty?

Sure. Kelly repeated.

Great. See you then.

Logan wasn't sure what to feel. Excitement? Fear? Dread? Was Kelly coming back into her life or telling her she was leaving forever? They were ridiculous thoughts, but Logan couldn't help it.

"What's going on in that head of yours?" Olivia asked.

Logan was too embarrassed to tell her the flip-flopping her brain was doing and how worried she was. "I'm not sure what to think."

"Why?"

"What if she wants to tell me she's done with me?"

"That's just crazy. Why would she agree to a boat ride if that was the case? I wouldn't want to be trapped on a floating thing in the middle of nowhere with someone I was going to break up with."

Logan hadn't considered that. "Okay. That makes me feel better."

"Of course, maybe she is planning on pushing you overboard. That would be quite the statement."

Logan shook her head. "I hate you sometimes. You know that?"

"I do. And I love you too." She put her hand on top of Logan's. "It's going to be okay. It really is."

"Thank you for that."

"What are you going to wear for your boat ride? You need to dress to impress."

"This isn't a date. I don't really know what it is. But definitely not a date." As much as she wished it was.

CHAPTER ELEVEN

Kelly felt sick to her stomach. She grabbed a light jacket and headed out the door to wait for Logan. She needed to find out what happened the night she got drunk. She couldn't think of anything else since waking up naked in Logan's bed.

She took a deep breath as she saw Logan's car round the corner and pull into the parking lot. The air was chilly and goose bumps erupted on her arms. She slipped her jacket on, glad she'd brought it. Logan leaned across the passenger seat to open the door for her.

"Hey there," Logan said.

"Hi." Kelly slipped on to the seat. "Thanks for picking me up."

"Of course. My pleasure."

Kelly wondered what else had been Logan's pleasure. She shuddered.

"Are you all right?"

"Yes. Just cold."

Logan turned the heat on. "Feel free to turn this off if you get too warm." This was the Logan Kelly had come to know. Kind. Caring. Not a person who would take advantage of someone who was drunk. But she had to be sure.

Logan pulled out onto the road and headed in the direction of the canal.

"Can I ask you a question and get an honest answer?" Kelly's plan hadn't been to start this conversation right away, but she needed to know and it couldn't wait any longer.

"Always."

Kelly closed her eyes and cleared her throat.

"What's going on, Kelly? Please talk to me."

Kelly looked at Logan, then turned her face away. She didn't want to look at her if her fears were true. "What happened the night I got drunk?"

"As far as I know you had four drinks…sex on the beach."

"That part I know. What happened after that? Up in your apartment."

"As soon as my shift was over, I helped you up the stairs. You had trouble walking. I got you to my bedroom, helped you out of your pants, and gave you a T-shirt to wear and went to get you a glass of water. You were in bed by the time I got back."

"And?"

"And that was about it. I shut off the lights and left the door open a crack in case you needed me."

"Did you…did we…?"

"Did we what?" She shook her head. "No, we didn't do anything. You were drunk. I would never ever do anything like that. I slept on the couch. I'm kind of hurt that you would even think that."

Kelly felt somewhat relieved but was not totally satisfied. "How did I end up naked?"

"You took your own clothes off when I went to get the water. I came back and you were under the covers with your clothes, including the T-shirt I had gotten you, thrown on the foot of the bed. I figured you were comfortable, so I just left." She paused. "Is this what the silent treatment was about? You thought I took advantage of you while you were drunk?" She shook her head. "Unbelievable. I thought you knew me better than that."

Kelly felt foolish. Not only had she worried over nothing, she hurt Logan by thinking the worst of her. "I'm sorry." She didn't know what else to say. Yes. She did know Logan, but all the evidence had told a different story. She never considered the possibility that she had taken her own clothes off unprompted.

"God, Kelly. I was so worried about you. Why the hell wouldn't you talk to me about this. Or better yet *know* that I wouldn't ever do anything like that. Christ. I can't believe this."

Kelly's thoughts went from the possibility of being a victim to being an ass in a split second. "I didn't know what to think. I couldn't imagine how I ended up with no clothes on and the bed…well, it looked like there had been a lot of action there." She didn't know how else to explain it.

"You must have had a restless night. I told you I slept on the couch. I didn't stand there and watch you sleep." The irritation was evident in Logan's voice.

Kelly wasn't sure how she could have ever thought such a thing about this wonderful woman. "I'm really sorry."

Logan didn't respond.

Shit. What had she done? And how could she make it better? "I'm sorry," she said again.

"Yeah. You've said that."

"What can I do to make it up to you?"

Logan just shook her head and bit her bottom lip.

This was bad. Kelly wasn't sure how they were going to get through the evening if she couldn't get Logan to forgive her.

They drove in silence until they were almost to the canal. "Why didn't you just talk to me instead of giving me the cold shoulder? I had no idea what the hell was going on with you, if I had done something to piss you off or what the problem was." She turned and looked at her. "Kelly, that was so wrong and so unfair."

"I know that now. I panicked. That's my only excuse. I've never gotten drunk before."

"Thank God, if that's the way you act after you do."

Yep. Logan was as mad as she could be. Maybe Kelly should be the one to suggest they put off the boat ride. She hesitated. Not sure if that would make Logan even angrier. "Do you think maybe we can stop somewhere and talk instead of going on the Riverboat?"

Logan pulled over, and for a minute Kelly thought she was going to tell her to get out. But that wasn't who Logan was. Even when she was this mad.

"Maybe we could go back to my apartment and talk?" Kelly raised her shoulders.

"I'm not sure what else there is to talk about. You think I'm capable of being a sexual predator."

"No."

"No? You weren't sure if we had sex while you were so drunk you could barely walk?"

"I know that if something had happened, I would have been a willing participant."

"You were way too out of it to give consent. Kelly, I respected you. I took care of you. I can't believe this."

"I know. I was wrong. I'm not used to someone looking after me. I've had to take care of myself from the time I could walk."

"That's not an excuse for thinking the worst of me. And ignoring my calls and texts." She put the car in drive and did a U-turn.

"It's the only excuse I have. I'm sorry that it's not good enough. I don't know what else to say. Are you bringing me home?"

"*You* said you wanted to talk there. Do you want to do that or not?" Logan attempted to keep her voice steady, but it came out harsher than she had intended.

"Yes," Kelly said in a quiet voice.

"Okay then." Logan didn't feel like going out on the Riverboat anymore, anyway. She wasn't sure what else there was to talk about. Kelly thought the worst of her and ghosted her over it. Where did you go from there?

They were silent on the short ride back to Kelly's apartment. Logan's mind was swirling as she climbed the stairs behind Kelly.

"Do you want something to drink?" Kelly asked.

Logan settled on the chair in the corner. "No."

Kelly got herself a glass of water and sat on the couch.

"Well?" Logan said. "What else did you want to say?" She knew she was being harsh, but she was mad. Damn it. And she had every right to be.

"I'm sorry," Kelly repeated.

"Let me ask you a question. Why did you break your own rule and have more than two drinks?"

Kelly seemed to think about it for several long beats before answering. "I've asked myself that repeatedly. I just wanted to stay and be around you, even if you were working. Drinking just seemed to be the thing to do."

"You wanted to be around me?" What exactly did that mean?

Kelly looked down and seemed to put her attention on her hands. She nodded. "I have feelings for you." She wiped a tear from the corner of her eye.

Feelings?

"I know that's ridiculous. You could never feel the same way about someone like me."

Kelly was wrong about that, but Logan was in no place to confess her own feelings. Her anger had overtaken them.

"Please say something," Kelly pleaded, finally making eye contact.

"I don't know what to say. What about Paula? You're over her just like that?" Logan snapped her fingers.

Kelly nodded. "I don't think I ever loved her. I just hung on because I didn't think I deserved better."

"Then how do you know your feelings for me are real if you couldn't tell your feelings for her weren't." Logan wasn't sure her question made sense. Her thoughts were so jumbled.

"I've come to know myself much better since meeting you. You see me. You know me. I think it gave me permission to really see myself and my worth."

She still didn't see her worth if she thought she was somehow lesser than Logan and thus not worthy of her love. But Logan wasn't about to press that point. There was still the fact that Kelly thought she was capable of taking advantage of her in a drunken state.

"Why the hell would you think the worst of me, Kelly? Do you know how much that hurts?"

"I don't know why."

"That answer isn't good enough. There has to be more."

Kelly took a drink of her water, taking her time to answer. "Before I met you, I'd heard rumors that you were only into one-night stands." She put up her hands. "Not that I was judging you. I was afraid I was just one more in a long line of many women."

"Women that I used?"

"That's not what I me—not used. But—"

"Let me assure you that every woman I've ever been with knew where I stood. I never tricked anyone or took advantage. And just for the record, I don't seek women out for sex. They proposition me. And I haven't said yes to any in a very long time. It's just not worth it." Probably more information than she needed to reveal.

"You haven't?"

"I haven't. And that has nothing to do with how you treated me or what you thought of me."

"Is there any way to make this up to you?"

"Nothing comes to mind." Logan didn't want to lose Kelly despite her hurt, but she wasn't willing to let her off the hook so easily. Not now. Not for a while. This sort of thing took time.

"I'm sorry. I'll be sorry until the day I die. Logan, you are so important to me. I panicked."

"And you jumped to conclusions instead of talking to me."

"I know that now. I tried to believe the best, but the way I woke up scared me." Tears streamed down her cheeks, and she made no attempt to wipe them away.

Logan resisted the urge to do it for her. "I did nothing but try to take care of you." The conversation was getting repetitive. There wasn't much more to say. "I'm going to go." She stood.

"Please don't." Kelly stood and reached for Logan's hand.

Logan pulled it away.

"Please don't hate me," Kelly said.

"See, that's the thing. I don't hate you. I never could. Maybe that makes this even worse." She made her way to the door knowing Kelly was staring after her. She hesitated with her hand resting on the doorknob. She had the urge to ease Kelly's distress but couldn't make herself do it. She opened the door and walked out.

Chapter Twelve

Logan drove to her sister's house and let herself in without knocking. She found Olivia sitting in her recliner, glued to the television. "Still watching *General Hospital*?"

Olivia jumped. She obviously hadn't heard Logan come in. "What are you doing here? I thought you had a date."

Logan sat on the couch. "It wasn't a date. And it didn't go too well."

"What happened? Did Kelly unfriend you?"

"Life isn't Facebook, Olivia."

"You know what I mean."

"She thought I took advantage of her while she was drunk. That's why she disappeared on me." Just saying the words out loud brought another round of anger as bile rose in Logan's throat. She went into the kitchen and poured herself a glass of water.

Olivia turned the TV off and followed her into the kitchen. "She thought the two of you had sex? How is that even possible?"

"She was really drunk. She didn't remember much of anything. I settled her down in my bed and I slept on the couch. But she didn't know that. She said she panicked when she woke up naked in my bed."

"Why was she naked? Did you undress her?"

"Oh my God, Olivia. Why does everyone think the worst of me? Why would I do that?"

"I don't know. To put her in pajamas?"

"I didn't." Logan explained how Kelly had shed her clothes.

"I can see why she was confused," Olivia said.

Logan took a large drink of her water trying to sooth the acid in her throat. "Confused is one thing. Blaming me for something that didn't happen is another."

Olivia leaned her back against the counter. "But can't you see her point? What would you think if the situations were reversed?"

"I might think that if I didn't know the other person, but she knows me. Why would she think that?"

"You two haven't actually known each other that long. I don't think it was an unreasonable conclusion."

Logan plopped down on a kitchen chair. "She has feelings for me." She rubbed the back of her neck. "I am so confused."

"If you think about this, her staying away from you makes sense."

"How so?"

"She has feelings for you. She drinks too much and wakes up naked in your bed. Of course, she's going to be scared. And if she's scared, she's going to keep her distance."

As much as Logan hated to admit it, that made sense. Fear could make people do extreme things. "What about the fact that she thought I could do that?" There were some things Logan still couldn't wrap her head around and wasn't ready to forgive.

"All evidence pointed to her jumping to that conclusion. What else was she supposed to think?"

"That I'm better than that."

"How do you know she has feelings for you?"

"She told me."

"Did you tell her it was mutual?"

"No way."

"Why?" Olivia pulled out a chair and sat across from Logan.

Logan shook her head. There was no way she was going to share that information with someone after they accused her of such heinous behavior. "And give her hope something could happen between us? No way."

"So, nothing could ever happen? You've let go of any thoughts of the two of you being together as a couple?"

Did she let that go? She didn't want to. She didn't know what she wanted. She was just so hurt. "I don't know."

"Don't throw away the possibility. You never know what it can be. You've been so anti-relationship since Judith hurt you. You've finally let your guard down."

"Yeah, and look where it got me?"

"That's not what I mean. It must take someone special for you to do that. Kelly must be special. Yes, she made a mistake. She's human. Cut her some slack."

Logan expected sympathy from Olivia, not for her to try to reason with Logan and defend Kelly. But some of what she was saying made sense. Up until a week ago Logan did think Kelly was pretty special. Was she willing to throw away a friendship with the possibly of more so easily? No not easily. Nothing about this was easy.

"Did you eat?" Olivia asked her. "Do you want to stay for dinner? Daniel is out getting Chinese food."

Logan didn't even want to think about eating. Her stomach flipped at the thought of food. "No. I'm going to get going. I just wanted to fill you in."

"And vent?"

"Yes. Thanks for listening to me. I appreciate it."

"Oh sure. I'm here for you."

Olivia's husband, Daniel, was coming in as Logan was going out. "Hey, sis-in-law. You're just in time for Chinese." He held up two large paper bags. "You're not leaving, are you?"

"I am. Rough day."

"Sorry to hear that. Nothing cures bad days like good food."

Olivia had certainly found a winner when she met Daniel. Logan couldn't ask for a better partner for her sister. She'd given up hoping to find that for herself a long time ago. Kelly had woken up a part of her that she thought was long dead. Now she didn't know if she should let it thrive or bury it once and for all.

"Thanks. But I'm going to pass. Rain check."

"You got it." He set the bags down on the counter and gave Olivia a kiss on the cheek. One more thing that Logan loved about him. He was never afraid to show his love for Olivia. Yes. She did want something like that. Maybe the dream wasn't as dead as she thought.

She said her good-byes and headed home to Bear. Bear. If nothing else, Logan would always be grateful to Kelly for giving him to her. She could have asked for him back after the fiasco with Paula, but she didn't. She wasn't that kind of person. Of course, Logan didn't think she was the kind of person to do what she had done either. She needed more time to figure out just what kind of a person she was.

❖

Kelly called Rachel as soon as Logan left. "I didn't sleep with her, but I practically accused her of taking advantage of me."

"Oh wow. Bet that didn't go over too good," Rachel responded.

"That's the understatement of the year. And, Rachel...I admitted I had feelings for her. I can't believe I did that."

"What did she say?"

"She asked about my feelings for Paula and how I could know if my feelings for her were real when my feelings for Paula weren't." Kelly filled her in on the rest of the conversation. "She was so mad, Rachel. I don't know what to do. I don't want to lose her. I don't hold any fantasies about a relationship, but I want to keep her as a friend. Between what I did and her knowing I have feelings, I'm not sure that's possible."

"I'm at a loss for words here. I'd tell you not to worry, but I don't know if this is fixable."

Kelly made her way into the bathroom and grabbed a wad of toilet paper to wipe her eyes and blow her nose. She closed the toilet lid and sat down. "That's what I'm thinking. She hates me. There's no way around that. I not only lost her. I lost Bear all over again. I blame Paula for this. All of it. If she hadn't deceived me, I probably wouldn't have thought the worst of Logan."

"Do you really think Logan would stop you from seeing Bear?"

"How can I go over there and face her again? Even if she let me, I don't think I can."

"Oh, Kelly, I'm so sorry. You don't deserve this."

"That's the kicker. I do deserve it. I'm the one who caused this."

"You didn't know."

"But I didn't ask either. I pulled back. I didn't give her a chance to explain anything. That's on me."

"What can I do to help?"

"Nothing. I'm grateful you're there for me. I'm going to go for a walk or take a shower. I don't know what to do with myself."

"Do you want to come over? Guess going to the Queen of Hearts is out."

"Probably forever. No. I think I would be very bad company right now."

"Don't worry about that. Mark is out practicing with his bowling team. I've got the house to myself."

"I'm going to pass. But thanks. I'll be okay. Eventually."

"You will, sweetie. You've come a long way. You'll get through this."

They said their good-byes and Kelly hung up. She turned on the water in the shower and then turned it off. She went to her room and threw herself on the bed. She fought back the tears that threatened but some leaked through anyway. She couldn't get Logan out of her mind. She'd done a lot of stupid things in her life, but this was probably the worst. Even stupider than believing Paula for almost nine months. She hurt Logan and that was unforgivable. She needed a way to fix this.

❖

It had been almost a week since Logan had seen or talked to Kelly. As much as she hated to admit it, she missed her. Her anger had settled down to a low roar. More of a small throbbing ache than actual pain. She thought the only way to get it gone for good was to forgive Kelly. Not only forgive her for her own sake but forgive her for Kelly's sake as well. She was sure Kelly was suffering as much as she had been.

She still had an hour before her shift at the bar. She pulled her phone from her pocket and settled down on the couch next to Bear. He laid one paw across her leg. "You think I should forgive her too, huh?"

Logan pulled up Kelly's contact information and typed out a text. *I start work in an hour. Drinks are on me if you want to come over. You can invite Rachel too if you want.* She reread it three times before hitting send. She wasn't sure if she should have explained how she was feeling or not. She just wanted to open the door to invite Kelly back into her life. Now it was in Kelly's court.

She didn't have to wait long for a response. *Rachel's busy, but I'll stop by. I'm only drinking water. I'm never drinking alcohol again. I'm a cheap date now.* She included a green-faced, vomiting emoji.

I'll buy you all the water you can drink, Logan responded. Okay, she did it. She reached out and Kelly reached back.

Why was she suddenly nervous? She didn't get nervous. What the hell?

She made herself a ham sandwich, wolfed it down, and brushed her teeth before changing her clothes for work. Bear was asleep on the couch when she let herself out the door and headed downstairs.

There weren't very many people in the bar, but Logan knew that it would fill up fast. Saturday evening was their busiest time. Helen was just finishing her shift and Joe was due to arrive at any moment.

Apron on, sleeves rolled up, Logan grabbed a clean bar rag and proceeded to wipe out glasses. She wasn't a fan of idle time. It made her shift seem so much longer. To her surprise, she watched Rachel come in and make her way over to the bar.

"Hey there," Logan said. "Kelly said you weren't coming. What can I get you?"

"Nothing. I'm not staying. I wanted to talk to you about Kelly," Rachel said.

"Ookaay," Logan said, dragging out the word.

"She told me what happened between the two of you. I'm not sure how much she's told you, but that girl has had a rough life."

Logan nodded.

"I don't think she can take much more pain. She doesn't deserve any more."

"I don't plan on causing her any pain, if that's what you're worried about." Logan appreciated Rachel's concern for her friend but didn't like that she was implying Logan's intentions were anything but pure.

"I don't think you would intentionally. She has feelings for you. You know that. I'm guessing you have feelings for her as well. I'm asking you to tread lightly. Don't give her any false hope if there isn't any."

"False hope?"

"For a relationship with you. I don't know for sure how you feel about her, and I'm not going to ask. Just be careful with her heart. Please."

"Message received."

"Thanks. Please don't tell Kelly I was here."

"As long as she doesn't ask, I won't volunteer it. But I won't lie." *For you or for anyone.*

"That's all I ask. Logan, Kelly is the best. She just doesn't know it. But I have the feeling you do."

"I do," Logan said. And she did. She watched Rachel as she weaved her way through the tables and out the door.

"Women trouble?" Joe said coming up behind her.

Logan laughed. "When have you ever known me to have trouble with a woman?" Other than Judith.

"Good point. Never. They'd be lined up around the block for you if you showed any interest."

"I'm trying to keep the sidewalks clear," Logan responded. "That's the only reason I don't."

"You're so civic-minded," Joe said. "I like that."

"Just doing my part."

It was a few hours before Logan saw Kelly come in and her heart did a little flip. She scooped some ice into a glass, filled it with water, and clipped a lemon slice on the rim. She set it down in front of Kelly as she slipped onto the only empty stool at the bar.

"Hi," Logan said.

"Hi."

"I've missed you," Logan said.

"Me too."

"I'm glad you're here."

"Me too." Kelly lifted her glass. "Thank you."

"Of course. How have you been?" They were both being way too formal, and it felt more than a little awkward.

"I've been better. Hard week. You?"

"Me too. I'm sorry."

"Me too." They both burst out laughing. "I'm not sure how many more times we can say *me too*."

"I've got at least a couple more in me," Logan said.

"Me too," Kelly responded. "Logan, I'm so sorry."

"I think we both said things we regret. And I may have overreacted the tiniest bit." She held up her hand, her thumb and forefinger nearly touching.

"Me too."

"Okay, no more with the *me too* stuff. There was no #MeToo Movement going on here. I think we've already established that."

Someone a few seats down flagged Logan over. "Be right back," she said to Kelly.

Kelly was surprised when she'd received Logan's text. She half expected to never hear from her again. Maybe more than half. She jumped at the chance to see her and was relieved when Rachel said she couldn't join her. She did wish that it was a more intimate—no, not intimate—private was a better word—setting. But this was a start. Maybe a neutral space being surrounded by strangers was a better idea.

"Hey, beautiful. Come here often?" She had noticed the bearded man, who was now practically leaning over her, approach.

"Is that your best opening line?" she asked him. "It's kind of lame."

"Oh yeah. What line should I start with?" His breath smelled liked he'd been indulging for quite a while.

"How about something like…I don't mean to bother you, so I won't?"

"That's not going to get me anywhere."

"Exactly."

He slipped onto the barstool next to her, practically sitting on the guy who was vacating it in the process. "Oh, don't be like that. I'm a nice guy. Let me buy you a drink. What are you drinking? Is that vodka?"

"What if I told you I'm not into nice guys?"

"I can run with that. You're looking for a bad boy?"

"Not looking for a boy at all," she said.

"How about a bad man? I can be as bad as you want." This guy was relentless.

"Really. Not. Interested."

"Come on, baby. I don't see no wedding ring. What's stopping you?" He put his hand over hers. She shook it off only to have him replace it.

"Hey." Logan was back. "Mind getting your grubby hand off my girlfriend?" she said to him.

Kelly was thankful for the save, although having Logan call her her girlfriend was a little shocking, even though Kelly knew she'd said it to get the creep to leave her alone.

"Aren't you supposed to be nice to the customers?" he asked her.

"Aren't you supposed to respect women and not be touching where you aren't welcomed?" She picked up his hand, moved it off Kelly's, and dropped it several inches away from her. "Need to wash this guy's scud off of you, honey?" she said to Kelly. "Come on in the back room and I'll help you with that."

"Damn dykes," he said, under his breath but loud enough for them to hear.

"Joe," Logan called. "This gentleman needs an escort out. Can you help him with that?"

Joe was several inches taller and a whole lot of muscle heavier than the jerk harassing Kelly. The guy put up his hands as soon as Joe started over. "I'm going. Don't like the service in this place anyway."

"You okay?" Logan asked Kelly as soon as he was gone. "What a jerk."

"Yeah. Thanks for the save."

"Sure." She turned serious for a moment. "You know, Kelly, I would do just about anything for you."

Kelly swallowed hard. There hadn't been too many times in her life that someone had said something like that to her. In fact, she wasn't sure anyone else ever had. Sure, Rachel and Marley were great friends, but this seemed like a whole different level of friendship. "Thank you. *Me too.*" Kelly laughed and Logan joined in.

"I have a fifteen-minute break coming up. Want to run upstairs with me and say hello to Bear?"

"I would like that." She hadn't been in Logan's apartment since waking up naked in her bed. She was upset when she left that morning. She was excited to be returning to the scene of the crime. Not that there was a crime. They had cleared that misunderstanding up—thank God.

"Joe," Logan said. "Back in fifteen. You got this?"

He gave her a half-hearted salute.

"Come on," she said to Kelly and lifted the piece at the end of the bar to keep the patrons from going in the back.

Kelly followed her through the back of the bar, out the door, and up the stairs. Logan took off her apron and tossed it over the back of a chair. Bear wasn't in the living room. "Probably in the bedroom," Logan said. "I'll go get him." She returned with the cat in her arms. "See," she whispered loudly in his ear. "I told you it was a good surprise." She deposited him safely in Kelly's arms. "Go ahead and sit," she said to Kelly. "You can make yourself at home when you're here. You don't need to act on formalities."

Kelly sat. It felt so good to see Bear again. Almost as good as it had been to see Logan. "I've missed you, little man," she said.

"Me too," Logan said in a quiet, squeaky voice, pretending it was Bear's.

Kelly laughed and whispered in Bear's ear. "We aren't allowed to say *me too* anymore."

"Yeah, Bear," Logan said. "Ease up." She sat down next to them. "Should we talk about what happened or do you think we covered it well enough?" she asked Kelly.

Kelly thought about it for a few seconds. She'd said she was sorry repeatedly. She knew what had actually happened. Logan had contacted her first, so she thought things were probably okay on her end. She wasn't sure there was any ground left to cover. "I'm good, if you're good."

"Then we're both good. Let's not go through anything like that again. It wasn't nearly as fun as I thought it would be."

"Fun?"

"I'm kidding. Remember, I'm a kidder?"

"Oh yeah. That's you. The kidder. I don't want a repeat performance either. I will do my best to remember how wonderful you are at all times."

"That's the way to do it." She paused. "Speaking of how wonderful I am...do you want to talk about feelings?"

Kelly wasn't prepared for that question. She wished she had never said anything or that they could just pretend the conversation never happened. "Not really."

"Why?"

Kelly ran her hand down Bear's back. He looked up and blinked at her as if he was waiting for an answer too. "Because."

"My mother used to tell us when we were kids that *because* is not an answer."

"My mother used to tell me—" She stopped. "Nothing good."

"I know. That had to be hard. Kelly, this doesn't have to be."

"I never should have said anything about my feelings. Some things are best left unsaid." You avoid a lot of awkwardness that way.

"I'm glad you said it."

That took Kelly by surprise. Logan seemed to be full of surprises today. "You are?"

Logan nodded. "Yeah. I'm glad you said it *first*. Because I was too chicken to."

"Too chicken to tell me that you knew about my feelings?" She thought she'd kept her feelings well hidden. She must have failed.

Logan shook her head. "No, silly. I'm trying to tell you that I have feelings for you as well."

Wait. What? What kind of feelings? Feeling feelings? Kelly was too afraid to ask.

"No response? I was hoping for at least a smile. Unless you've changed your mind. Is that it? Have you changed your mind or have your feelings changed?"

"No."

"Kelly, this is like pulling teeth here and I have a fear of dentistry."

"You're afraid of being a dentist?"

"Kelly."

"I'm not sure of what you are trying to tell me. I'm sorry."

Logan took her hand. "I'm trying to say I like you."

That much Kelly already figured.

"*Like you* like you. Like more than like you."

"You more than like me? You have feelings too?" That was more than Kelly could comprehend in the moment. How could someone as great as Logan like—more than like—someone like her? She knew if she voiced that, Logan would tell her to stop putting herself down.

"Yes," Logan said. "I have feelings for you."

"How?"

"What the hell kind of a question is that? How do I have feelings? Do you want me to tell you all the ways I think you're wonderful? Because I'm more than willing." She glanced at the clock near the TV. "But I'll have to do it fast because my break is almost over."

"No, that won't be necessary." Logan felt for her the same way she felt for Logan. That's all she needed to know.

"You probably wouldn't believe half of it anyway. Would you?"

"I'm working on it."

"Good. I've got to get back to work. Do you want to come back down? Or you can stay up here with Bear if you want."

"It's okay to stay up here where creeps aren't hitting on me?"

"I want to be the only creep that hits on you. Wait. That didn't come out right." She laughed. "I want to talk about this more, but I really do have to go. Would it be okay if I gave you a kiss before I do?"

Kelly had actual dreams about moments like this, but never thought in a million years it would really happen. She turned toward Logan and nodded.

"Yes? I want to be sure. Don't want to be accused of taking advantage."

Kelly swatted her arm. "Shut up and kiss me." She was wet with anticipation.

Logan took Kelly's face in both her hands, leaned in, and gave her a gentle kiss on the lips. She pulled back and looked into Kelly's eyes. "Okay?" she asked.

"Kind of lame," Kelly said. "I think you can do better."

Logan pulled her in and kissed her again, harder, longer, deeper. They were both out of breath when they came up for air. "Better?"

Kelly wasn't sure she could take a better kiss and remain conscious. It was by far the best kiss she'd ever had. "Holy shit."

"I'll take that as a yes," Logan said. "Damn. I really have to go. Damn. I really don't want to." She gave Kelly another quick kiss on the lips.

She got up and started for the door. "Stay as long as you want or come back down to the bar if you want."

"Wait," Kelly said.

"You want another kiss, don't you?" Logan asked her.

"I do, but I stopped you because you forgot your apron."

"Oh." Logan grabbed the apron, kissed Kelly on the top of her head, and went out the door, closing it behind her.

Kelly stared at the door, not fully believing what had just happened. If it wasn't for the tingle on her lips and the dampness of her underwear, she would have thought she'd fantasized the whole thing. Logan had kissed her and this time she meant it. She leaned back and closed her eyes. Logan liked her. Really, really liked her. Wow. Just Wow.

CHAPTER THIRTEEN

Logan hadn't planned on telling Kelly about her feelings, much less kiss her, so soon. But found she couldn't help herself when they were alone in her apartment.

"What's the grin for?" Joe asked her.

"Life," she said. "Life is looking up."

"Good to hear. Glad you're back. Life here has gotten really busy."

Logan had been so lost in her own head she hadn't realized just how many more people were in the bar. Several tables had been pushed together for some sort of celebration. Looked like a birthday party from the number of gifts piled on the tables.

Logan didn't stop moving for the next hour and a half. There would have been no way to spend any time with Kelly if she'd come back down. She was comforted by the fact that Kelly was up in her apartment spending time with Bear.

"Hi. Can I get a rum and Coke?" an attractive woman asked Logan.

"You got it."

"Can I buy you a drink?" the woman asked when Logan set her drink in front her. "Maybe when your shift ends."

Logan smiled. She was used to getting hit on by women and occasionally men. "I appreciate that, but no thank you."

The woman slipped a piece of paper in her hand along with cash for the drink. "My number, if you change your mind."

Logan wadded up the piece of paper as soon as the woman returned to the birthday group. She turned just in time to see Kelly, who must have come in from the back.

"Does that happen often?" Kelly asked.

"What?"

"Women hitting on you? Giving you their phone numbers?"

"All the time. Day and night. It gets so tiring."

"I can only imagine," Kelly said with a smile.

It was that smile that first drew Logan in. "Hi."

"Hi," Kelly responded. "I'm going to get going. I didn't want to leave without saying good-bye."

"What do you say we try again for that Riverboat ride? Tomorrow's my day off, as you know."

"That sounds like a plan."

"Pick you up at four thirty?"

Kelly nodded. "I think we can do it right this time."

"I'm counting on it," Logan said. "Care to step into the back room with me for a minute before you leave?"

Kelly looked around at the crowded bar. "Is that allowed? Aren't you wicked busy?"

"We are, but I can take a sixty-second break." She paused. "If you're agreeable."

"Lead the way."

The kiss they shared in the back room left Logan breathless, making it hard to concentrate when she returned to her place behind the bar.

Kelly gave a final wave as she disappeared through the crowd out the front door. Logan stared after her, until a customer pulled her attention.

"What can I get you?"

"I'll have whatever you're having. That is one incredible smile on your face."

Logan didn't realize she was smiling, but only had Kelly to blame. "Sorry," she said. "You'll have to settle for a drink. The woman that put this smile on my face is all mine." At least she hoped she was.

❖

"I feel like I'm floating," Kelly said.

"Umm, that might be because we're on a boat," Logan responded.

"I don't think it's that." She settled back against Logan.

"What else could it be?" Logan wrapped her arms around Kelly. There was a slight chill in the air, but Kelly kept her warm.

They'd gotten to the boat early and were the first ones on. They chose a spot standing by the railing instead of claiming any of the seats toward the center of the boat. Other people were slowly filing on, filling up the seats and spaces around them.

"You okay with this? PDA?"

Kelly turned in Logan's arms, faced her, and planted a light kiss on her lips. "I hate it."

"I can tell." Logan kissed her back. "You're going to miss the scenery if you stay in this position."

"Oh, but the scenery is so much nicer like this."

"All aboard," a stray voice called out. A deep horn blasted from somewhere toward the front of the boat and they started moving, pulling away from the dock.

It was much smoother than Logan expected it to be. "Deer," she said.

Kelly looked up at her. "Yes?"

"No. Turn around. There's a deer." She pointed to the left, thick with trees and plant life. The right side of the canal boasted a paved walking and biking trail.

Kelly turned around, staying within the confines of Logan's arms. "Aww. That's so cool. Look. She has a baby." A fawn came out from between two trees and started munching on the same vegetation its mother was eating.

"Tell me some deer trivia," Logan said.

"You think I have this stuff just bouncing around in my head, ready to call up at a moment's notice?" Kelly paused. "The males' antlers fall off every year and regrow in the spring."

Logan hugged her tighter. "I knew you would have some interesting tidbit. I don't think I've ever known anyone as smart as you."

"I'm not sure having a head full of useless information qualifies me as being smart."

"Hey," Logan said. "That so-called useless information got us this boat ride and dinner for two. How about we go out to dinner on Wednesday?"

"I would like that. I'm always up for a free meal," Kelly said. She pointed out a family of ducks as they swam by, far enough from the boat to stay safe.

"Turns out your useless information wasn't so useless after all."

"You came up with some answers too. It wasn't all me. I didn't have a clue about that basketball question."

"Me either. It was a lucky guess."

"I'm the lucky one," Kelly said. "I never dreamed this was possible."

"A boat ride on the canal? Totally possible. Three times a day. Five on weekends."

Kelly elbowed her. "You. I never dreamed *you* were possible."

"I'm right here. And I'm very possible."

Kelly closed her eyes and raised her chin, letting the sunlight and contentment wash over her. She still felt like she was in a dream. They hadn't talked about the future or where they thought this was heading, and she was okay with that. She just wanted to enjoy each moment she had with Logan.

"There's a bar inside," Logan whispered in her ear, sending chills down her back. "Want me to buy you a drink?"

"Ugh," Kelly said. "No. The last drink I had got me in all kinds of trouble."

"The three you had before that one may have played a part too."

"Four."

"Huh?"

"I *think* I had a total of five drinks."

"I remember giving you four and thinking that might be overdoing it."

"I got one from Joe too."

"No wonder you couldn't remember anything the next morning."

"Yeah. Never again. If and when I do go back to drinking, I'm sticking to two sloe gin fizzes. Is it fizz or fizzes? That's hard to say."

"So, no more sex on the beach?" Logan asked.

Kelly turned her head just enough that she could see Logan out of the corner of her eyes. "Not the drink. Not saying actual sex on the beach is out." She had never been this forward or confident with anyone before. She was surprising even herself.

"Are you threatening me with a good time?"

"I'm promising you a good time."

"Kelly," Logan said, her tone turning serious. "I want to take my time with this. Do it right. Can you understand that?"

Kelly nodded.

"I want this to work," she continued. "You mean the world to me." She kissed the back of Kelly's neck.

Kelly closed her eyes against the sensations rushing through her. Going slow was a good idea. At least her brain thought so. Her body had other ideas. "Ditto. You mean the world to me as well. No one has ever treated me as good as you do."

"You're worth it. More than worth it."

"Look," Kelly said. "An eagle's nest. Oh my God, look how big that bird is."

"Wow. I've never seen one in the wild before. That is so cool." Almost as if on cue, the bald eagle took off in flight leaving three or four babies bobbing up and down in the nest. "Ahh. Amazing."

The captain came on the loudspeaker announcing the presence of the eagle, babies, and nest. The people around them turned to discover what Kelly and Logan had already seen.

"Has he been making announcements the whole time?" Kelly asked.

"I think so. I haven't been paying attention. For some reason I've been more interested in the woman in my arms."

"Me?"

"You."

They saw several herons and other wildlife, while the captain, or whoever was doing the narrating, spouted facts and anecdotes about the canal and its surrounding area, pointing out interesting sights and animals as they traveled across the water. The ninety-minute tour was over before they knew it.

They followed the other passengers exiting the boat single file. Once back on the dock, Logan took Kelly's hand, intertwining their fingers. "Want to go for a walk?"

"Sure."

They walked the path in the opposite direction the boat had taken them. They encountered far fewer people on the trail than were on the boat. Logan pointed out a bunny, various birds, including a pair of cardinals, the male brighter than any Kelly had ever seen.

When a snake slithered across the path Logan stopped and pulled Kelly back. "Shit. Snake."

"What? Where?"

"Did I ever tell you I'm terrified of snakes?" Logan said.

"As a matter of fact, you didn't. That's just a garter snake. He's harmless."

"Not if he gives me a heart attack." They waited for several long seconds after the snake had disappeared into the underbrush before continuing. Logan kept a watchful eye on the area he had crawled into. "How do you know so much about snakes? Probably stupid question. You know so much about everything."

"I took a few night classes centered around animals. People were always disappointing me. Animals seemed like they would be better friends."

"I'm so sorry. Some people suck, that's true. But not everyone."

"I know. I've got Rachel and Marley and now you. My life has gotten so much better since then."

Logan squeezed her hand. They walked for a little while in comfortable silence, with the sounds of the birds, frogs, and an occasional fish splash filling the gaps. They didn't notice right away when the sun ducked behind a cloud and the sky turned from bright blue to an ominous shade of gray. It wasn't until the first raindrops landed on Kelly's face that she realized the sudden change in the weather.

They looked around for some form of shelter on the open trail. A short way ahead there was an information board with maps of the area trails. A small roof of sorts stuck out about a foot and a half on the front and back.

They made their way to it just before the sky opened up and the rain came down in buckets, hitting the paved path so hard that it splashed up, soaking the bottom of their pants. "I've always wanted to dance in the rain with someone special," Kelly said.

Logan stepped out from under the tiny roof and put her hand out to Kelly. Kelly pulled her back under. "Are you crazy? I said in the rain. Not a monsoon. You are soaking wet now."

"I did it for you. The least you could do is put your arms around me to warm me up."

Kelly pulled Logan close and wrapped her arms around her, her shirt soaking up some of the rain from Logan's clothes. She didn't care. She pulled Logan's face down to hers and kissed her gently at first and then with more passion and determination. She went weak in the knees when Logan's tongue slipped between her lips.

Kelly ran her fingers through Logan's wet hair and down the back of her shirt, bringing them back up *under* Logan's shirt once she'd reached the bottom.

Logan's skin under her fingertips felt so soft, so smooth, so delicious. It was a sensation Kelly wanted to commit to memory. She wanted to memorize every inch of this beautiful creature before her. Touching Logan, even someplace so innocent as her back, was doing things to Kelly's body that she'd never experienced before. She couldn't believe how on fire her body felt. Every cell was standing at attention.

She wasn't sure how much more she could take without exploding. Kissing and touching Logan was more sensual and sexual then having actual sex with past partners. How was that even possible?

Kelly suddenly pulled out of the kiss and stepped out from under the overhang into the pouring rain.

"What are you doing?" Logan asked, a shocked look on her face.

"Cooling off. You make me hot, woman."

"Get over here." Logan pulled her out of the rain by her arm. "You don't need me to make you hot. You're hot all by yourself."

Kelly laughed. "Not this kind of hot. I could never get this hot by myself. And believe me I've tried." She put her hand over her mouth. "Too much information."

"Wow. I'm learning all kinds of new things about you. I like it."

"I didn't mean to say that. Let's forget I did."

"Oh no. Too late. I'm filing that little visual away in my brain for later."

"For later? What are you planning on doing with it?"

"Never you mind." Logan looked up. "The rain's starting to let up."

"Way to change the subject."

"You didn't want to talk about this anyway. Should we wait for it to stop completely or head back now?"

"Let's wait a little bit. I'm enjoying just being here with you. Are you okay with that?"

"Being here with you a little while longer? You bet I am."

The rain stopped completely about fifteen minutes later, and the sun came back out as if it had never left. They walked back to the dock hand in hand. And Logan drove them back to Kelly's apartment.

"I would invite you up," Kelly said. "But we are going to take it slow, and I can't promise that if you come up with me."

"I totally understand," Logan replied. "I had a great time today."

"I did too. Thank you so much."

"Don't thank me. It was mostly your incredible brain that won us the tickets."

"True," Kelly said with a laugh.

Logan pulled back a little and raised one eyebrow. "Did I just hear you take a compliment and agree that you have an incredible brain?"

"I'm trying."

"You're doing great." Logan leaned over and kissed her. Softly at first, then with more intensity. She pulled out of the kiss with difficulty. "Slow," she said. "Taking it slow." She jumped out of the car and opened the passenger door before Kelly had a chance to.

"Why thank you," Kelly said.

Logan walked her to the door that led up the stairs. She gave her a hug and a quick kiss. "Good night. We're on for Wednesday, but feel free to come over to the apartment or the bar if you feel like it in the meantime."

"Okay," Kelly said. "Good night. And thanks again."

Logan jumped back in her car as soon as Kelly closed the door behind her. She let out a sigh. "That girl's going to be the death of me," she said to herself. "In the best possible way."

She pulled out onto the road and pressed the Bluetooth button on her steering wheel. "Call Olivia," she said.

"Hello."

"Hi, sis," Logan said.

"What's up? You seem like you're in a really cheerful mood."

"You can tell that just from me saying *hi*?"

"Actually yeah."

"Kelly and I just got back from the Riverboat ride. It was nice. Really nice."

"Kelly? I didn't know you were back to doing things with her. Does that mean you forgave her?"

"I did. I realized my life is better with her in it." Logan opened her window a crack to let in some of the early evening air.

"From what you've told me about her, I agree. What else? I know there's more to this."

"What are you psychic now?"

"I know you," Olivia said.

"I told her on Saturday that I have feelings as well. We're taking it slow, but we want to see where this goes."

"You told her on Saturday and you're calling to tell me now? What the hell?"

"Hey. Take what you can get."

"So, this was an actual date?"

"It was." Logan pulled onto the expressway.

"And you're absolutely giddy."

"I don't get giddy."

"Logan, you're giddy. It's not a bad thing. It's actually pretty great. It's about time you found someone worthy of you."

"She's so great, Olivia."

"I can tell. When do I get to meet her?"

"It's all about you, isn't it?"

"Yep."

"We'll figure something out. But not yet. I want her all to myself for a while." They continued to talk until Logan pulled into the parking lot behind the bar. "I'm home. Wanted to catch you up," Logan said.

"I'm happy for you, Logan. You deserve the best. Love you."

"Thanks. Love you too. Bye."

Logan made her way up the stairs and into her apartment. Bear was stretched on the couch. She plopped down next to him and ran a hand over his back. "I think I'm crazy about her, Bear."

He didn't bother asking her who. He must have known she was talking about Kelly. "Of course, I'm talking about Kelly. Mama Kelly to you. Have you eaten? I should probably eat something. I should have gotten food for Kelly before I brought her home. What the hell was I thinking."

Bear just stared at her and laid a paw across her lap. "I know I wasn't thinking with my stomach. Don't judge me." At that her stomach growled. "Okay, okay. I'll feed you." Bear jumped off the couch as soon as Logan stood up. He ran to his food bowl. "Don't tell me you're out of food. The bowl was full when I left."

His bowl was half full but there was a small portion of the bottom of the bowl showing. She picked it up and shook it to spread the food around. Bear leaped for it as soon as she put it down. "You poor baby. You must have been starving, I mean only having half a bowl of food."

She opened the refrigerator to see what she had. Nothing looked particularly appealing. She peered into a plastic container and threw out something she couldn't identify. "Grilled cheese," she said. "Fast. Simple. Filling." She hummed as she buttered the bread, added cheese, and put it in the frying pan.

Bear ate a little more of his food and sat, staring up at her. "What? Never seen a happy person before?" And she was. Happy. She couldn't wait for Wednesday, but she hoped she would see Kelly again before that.

CHAPTER FOURTEEN

K elly looked at herself in the mirror and applied more eyeliner. Several layers of eye shadow, mascara, and blush later, she was satisfied. Mascara and a little eye liner was all she usually wore, and she didn't even do that very often. She wrestled with the curling iron for almost twenty minutes before she was fairly happy with her hair. Mist filled the air as she sprayed it into place. She stepped out of the bathroom to let the air settle, stepped back in, and applied another layer.

She changed into the outfit she'd bought just for this date with Logan. She tugged at the hem of her dress and admired herself in the full-length mirror. The blue-and-gold flowered pattern wasn't something she would have normally picked out— hell, wearing a dress wasn't something she would have normally done, but she wanted to look extra nice.

She finished getting ready a few minutes before Logan knocked. A bouquet of flowers greeted her when she opened the door. They were beautiful, but not as beautiful as the woman holding them.

"For you," Logan said.

"Thank you. I love them. Come on in. Let me find a vase." She opened every cabinet door in the kitchen, hoping against hope that she had something decent to put them in and finally settled on an oversize beer mug.

"Umm," Logan said. "You're wearing a dress."

"And pantyhose." Kelly tugged at the waist band. She wasn't sure how women wore such things on a regular basis.

"Are you comfortable in them? Both I mean. The dress and the pantyhose. I've only seen you in pants. Be honest."

Kelly briefly considered glossing over the truth but decided deception in any form wasn't a good idea. "Not really."

"Why don't you take them off?"

"A...well...I thought you wanted to go slow. Not that I'm objecting..."

A blush colored Logan's cheeks. "No. I mean change into something you're comfortable in. Kelly, I appreciate all the effort you put into getting ready, but...can I be totally honest with you?"

"Of course." She wouldn't want it any other way.

"I really like you the way you are. Little or no makeup. Pants, even jeans if that's more comfortable. And your hair, natural. I mean if you were comfortable and felt better this way then that's how I would want you to be. But you're not. I just want you to be you. I don't want you to try to change for me. Even for a date."

"But you look great. You always look great."

"I put on clean pants and a button-down shirt instead of jeans and a T-shirt. But this is still me." Logan paused and seemed to choose her words carefully. "I want you to be you. I like you. The real you. You're beautiful just the way you are."

Kelly wasn't sure what to think. Logan was right. This wasn't her, but no one she ever dated wanted the real her. This was all new. "You want me to change and take off some of my makeup?" She tugged at the waistband of her pantyhose again.

Logan took her hand. "Only if that's what you want to do. I hope I'm explaining this right. I'll take you any way you are, but please just be you. The *you* I'm crazy about. I'm sorry. I shouldn't have said anything. You went out of your way to get ready. We should go."

"No. I'm glad you said something. I wanted to look nice for you. But you're right. This isn't me. I'm not sure anyone I ever went out with liked me just the way I am. I tried to fit into the mold of who they were looking for."

"They were wrong. Kelly, don't change for me. Or anyone. You are so great, just the way you are. You've pulled at those pantyhose several times in the last two minutes. How do you think they'll feel a couple of hours from now?"

Kelly laughed. "Probably pretty bad. I'm going to go take them off. Do you mind waiting?"

"Of course not."

Kelly washed her face, reapplied a small amount of eye liner and mascara and brushed most of the hairspray out of her hair. It felt much better than that stiff mass that was there a few minutes ago.

She shed the dress and pantyhose. She breathed a sigh of relief and absently rubbed where the waistband had dug into her. She chose a pair of gray slacks and a pale pink button-down shirt. She rummaged through her sparse jewelry box and found a thin gold chain that she hooked around her neck.

She nodded at her reflection in the full-length mirror. This was much more her style, and Logan was right, she would be much more comfortable and have a more enjoyable evening than she would have had pretending to be someone she wasn't—even if it was only in how she looked.

Logan was settled down on the couch when Kelly returned. "I hope I didn't offend you. I just want you to be you and comfortable in your own skin."

"You didn't and I thank you for your honesty. You were right. This is much more me."

"I love the way you look, just the way you are."

"Thank you. I'm ready if you are."

Logan stood and opened her arms. "I need to kiss you first."

Kelly stepped into her. "Well, if you really feel you need to."

"I do," Logan said. She tipped her head down, cupped Kelly's chin, and kissed her lightly on the mouth.

Kelly would have liked a little more passion, but she knew if she pushed it, they would be very late for their reservations.

"That was a tiny preview," Logan said. "Much more to come." Logan took her hand and led her down to the car. She held the passenger door open for her and then slid into the driver's seat and kissed Kelly full on the mouth. Kelly's stomach clenched when Logan's tongue pressed between her lips and proceeded to explore. She was sure her underwear was damp by the time Logan pulled back.

"Sorry," Logan said. "I couldn't help myself."

"Umm. No problem. Feel free to do that anytime the spirit moves you." *And I hope it moves you often.*

Logan started the car. "Thanks. I appreciate your willingness to share your lips. Your lovely, luscious lips."

They didn't have to wait long at the restaurant for their table. Logan offered to get a bottle of wine for Kelly, but she passed. She wasn't ready to drink alcohol again, not as sick as she felt after her one drunken night.

"Order whatever you want," Logan said. "It's on me."

"Aren't our meals free seeing we won dinner for two as part of the trivia contest prize?"

"They are. I mean the gift certificate is *on* me. In my back pocket." She laughed.

"You're a goof, you know that?"

"I do. Some say it's my best feature."

"It is."

Kelly had never felt so comfortable with anyone before. Logan gave her permission to be herself. There were times when she didn't know who that was, but she was learning—and surprisingly liking the person she was discovering.

The food turned out to be almost as good as the company was. "Share dessert?" Logan asked.

"Absolutely. What should we get?"

Logan set the dessert menu down on the table. "Your choice. It all looks so good."

"Oh no. The pressure is on."

"No pressure. No pressure for anything. I mean that."

Kelly believed her. The only thing Logan had ever pressured her about was to be true to herself and not put herself down. She could live with that kind of pressure.

"How about..." Kelly tried to narrow down the choices. "Tiramisu cheesecake? That sounds so good."

Logan smiled and Kelly soaked up the feelings it stirred in her. "Excellent choice."

"That was so good," Kelly said, after taking the last bite, which Logan insisted was hers. "I'm full."

"It's still early. What else would you like to do? Movie? Dancing? Karaoke? Or we could go back to my place," Logan said.

"I vote for your place. I'm working on my self-confidence, but nowhere near ready for public dancing or karaoke."

"How about private dancing at my apartment?"

"I think I could handle that."

"Do you think we can control ourselves?"

"Do we have to?" Kelly asked. She was ready for the next step. It wouldn't exactly be *taking it slow*, but it wasn't like she and Logan hadn't known each other for a while now. But she was willing to wait if that's what Logan wanted.

Logan seemed to think about it for several long beats.

Kelly was sure she was going to say it was too soon. "Or not," she said, hoping to let Logan off the hook.

"How about we let things happen naturally? See where the evening takes us."

"I can live with that. Shall we take care of the check and make our exit?"

Logan gave the waiter the gift certificate for their meals along with a generous tip that she refused to let Kelly contribute to.

"Bear," Logan called out as they entered her apartment. "I'm home. And I brought company."

"Do you always announce your arrival to him," Kelly asked.

"Nope. But you're here. He needs to know it's a special evening." Logan hung her keys up on the hook by the door.

Kelly spotted Bear stretched out on the couch and ran a hand over his smooth fur.

"Would you like anything to drink? I got a bottle of wine in case you wanted it."

"Oh my gosh, that was so nice. Thank you. Just a glass of water would be good. But hang on to the wine. I'll get back into it at some point."

"So, I shouldn't throw the bottle out?"

"Smart-ass. No."

"You've been studying my ass? And it's smart. Next trivia contest we can ask my butt for some of the answers." Logan poured a glass of water and handed it to Kelly.

"Now that is a good idea. Give my brain a rest." She took a sip and set it down on a coaster.

"Alexa," Logan said to the device on the end table. "Play slow dance music."

The device lit up briefly and filled the room with sound.

"Shall we?" Logan offered a hand to Kelly.

Kelly wasn't very confident in her dancing abilities, but the anticipation of being so close to Logan eased her mind. She took the hand Logan offered and let Logan pull her in close. Logan wrapped both arms around her, letting one hand slip a little under the waistband of Kelly's pants. She loved the feeling of Logan's hand on her skin. "Can you lead?" Kelly whispered.

Logan nodded and placed her cheek against Kelly's.

To Kelly's relief, there were no complicated steps. Logan kept it simple, and Kelly had no problem keeping up. She closed her eyes and let their rhythm and heat from Logan's body envelop her. She wasn't sure she'd ever felt so comfortable and contented in her life.

Kelly wasn't sure if they'd been dancing for ten minutes or two hours, when Logan pulled back far enough to look into her eyes for what felt like forever, before leaning in and kissing her. Hard. Thoroughly. Completely. Every part of Kelly's mouth was involved, and her body reacted accordingly.

She sucked in a breath when Logan stroked her breast.

"Okay?" Logan whispered.

Kelly nodded, not sure anything would come out if she attempted to speak.

It took only a few moments for Logan's mouth to be on hers again and her hands to be under Kelly's shirt. She extracted her hand long enough to unbutton the shirt, one button at a time, agonizingly slow. Logan pushed the shirt back and moved her mouth from Kelly's mouth to her shoulder, placing small kisses and tongue flicks along her skin and up her neck.

Kelly tilted her head back, her body flooding with sensation and her underwear wet from her excitement. Her shirt landed on the floor and Logan unhooked her bra, slipping it off in the process.

Kelly ached for Logan to have her mouth on her breasts, and she didn't have to wait long for Logan to comply with Kelly's unspoken command.

Kelly's hands were in Logan's hair, holding her head in place as if Kelly was afraid she would run away. Logan's moans mixed with Kelly's until Kelly couldn't tell which sounds were coming from who.

Logan waltzed them into the bedroom and stripped off the rest of Kelly's clothes. Kelly could feel Logan's eyes on her.

"Beautiful," Logan whispered.

Kelly felt the heat rise in her body. She attempted to unbutton Logan's shirt, but Logan stepped back and stopped her.

Kelly asked a silent question with her eyes.

"I want…no…need…this to be about you. Not the whole time. Just for now."

Kelly blinked away the tears that filled her eyes. So much of this was new and unexpected.

Logan wiped a stray tear from Kelly's face with her thumb. "You okay?" she whispered.

Kelly nodded. She was more than okay. Much more.

Logan pulled down the covers and settled Kelly down on the edge of the bed. She knelt in front of Kelly and kept eye contact while she gently pushed her knees apart.

Kelly nodded again and Logan leaned in and kissed Kelly between her breasts. Kelly leaned forward, granting Logan full access and Logan wasted no time using her mouth to give Kelly's nipples the attention they craved, sending a surge of electricity though Kelly, landing squarely in her center causing another rush of moisture.

Logan worked her way down Kelly's body, licking and planting kisses along the way. Kelly closed her eyes, threw her head back, and let out a low moan as Logan's mouth made contact with her center. Logan's tongue swept over her most sacred place and entered her.

Kelly's brain released any thoughts as the sensations in her body increased and she reached the edge of an orgasm. A sudden and unexpected fear enveloped her. What if she couldn't climax and she disappointed Logan? She'd never had that thought or fear before. No one else ever seemed to care.

Logan must have sensed a change and pulled back.

Kelly opened her eyes and brought them to Logan's.

"Relax," Logan said. "Let it happen. We're together in this. I've got you."

Kelly tried to absorb Logan's words. She willed her body to relax and concentrated on the throbbing between her legs.

Logan slipped first one finger, then another into Kelly. Kelly gasped. "There you go," Logan said in a husky voice. "Let it go."

Kelly leaned back on her elbows and squeezed her eyes shut.

Logan added her tongue to the mix, and Kelly allowed herself to go over the edge. Her body jerked forward as bright colors burst behind her closed eyelids. She sucked in a large breath of air and held it as the waves that started in her center ripped through her and she collapsed back onto the bed.

Logan waited for several long moments before she took back possession of her fingers, climbed on the bed next to Kelly, and wrapped her arms around her. She snuggled into Kelly's neck. "How ya doing?"

Kelly was afraid that nothing would come out if she tried to talk. She opened her eyes and turned toward Logan.

"You're crying." Logan wiped tears that Kelly hadn't realized were there from the corners of her eyes. "Are you okay?"

Kelly nodded. "That was…it was…I mean…oh my God."

"Very well said."

Kelly tried to laugh, but it sounded more like a grunt. "Logan, that was amazing. You're amazing."

"Right back at'cha."

"What did I do that was so amazing? I didn't do anything."

"You let go when you were afraid. That takes courage and trust."

"I can't believe that happened. You were so great."

"You just needed to know it was okay. You were safe." Logan ran a single finger down Kelly's body, between her breasts to her belly button.

Kelly shivered at the contact.

"Cold?" Logan pulled the covers up around her.

"How come I'm the only one naked here?" Kelly asked.

"You want me naked?"

"I do."

Logan stood and slowly removed her clothes, letting each piece drop to the floor.

Kelly's arousal started all over again at the sight of her perfect body. She reached her arms out to Logan.

Logan crawled in bed next to Kelly and resumed her position with her arms around her. "Better."

Kelly couldn't believe how good it felt to be skin to skin with Logan. She felt content, protected, safe. And very turned on. "I think it's my turn to make you feel good."

"That can wait," Logan said. "I just want to lie with you like this for a while."

Kelly pulled back enough to look Logan in the face. "You're not one of those people that only gives and never receives, are you? I wouldn't like that."

Logan laughed. "Oh no. I'm good at receiving. Excellent in fact. But at the moment, I just want you in my arms."

Kelly snuggled in closer. "All right. I can deal with that. For now."

It wasn't long before she drifted off to sleep. It took her a minute when she woke up to figure out where she was. The rhythmic breathing next to her told her Logan had also fallen asleep. She considered waking her up but decided against it. She closed her eyes content to just be curled up against her.

Sunlight was streaming through the window when Kelly opened her eyes again.

"Hello, beautiful," Logan said.

Kelly blinked at her. "Were you watching me sleep?"

"Just for a little while. How are you doing? Happy? Contented?"

"Mostly," Kelly said.

"Just mostly? Not totally?"

"Not until I do this." Kelly claimed Logan's breast and ran her thumb over her nipple, feeling it stand at attention.

She replaced her thumb with her mouth, rolling her tongue around Logan's flesh, tasting the salty sweetness of her. Kelly walked her fingers down Logan's body, paused to circle her belly button, continued down, and slipped a single finger through Logan's folds.

The moan that escaped Logan's lips sent a surge of electricity through Kelly. "You're so wet," she said.

"See what you do to me?"

Kelly hooked a leg over Logan's and pulled it toward her to give her more access to explore with her fingers. She let the delicious sounds coming from Logan guide her. The rhythm of her breathing and moans became the rhythm of Kelly's fingers as she slipped them in and out of Logan, going deeper with each thrust.

The arms around her tightened as an orgasm ripped through Logan's body, clamping down on Kelly's fingers and then releasing them with pulsing contractions. Kelly waited until Logan's breathing settled down before extracting her fingers.

Logan pulled Kelly's face to hers and kissed her, her tongue taking possession of Kelly's mouth. She deepened the kiss and Kelly felt as if they were one. One mouth. One body. One soul.

"Happy now?" Logan asked when they came up for air.

"I am. Very. You?"

"Semi."

Kelly froze, afraid her efforts hadn't been enough.

Logan rolled on top of her, wiggling her hips, until Kelly's legs parted. She settled in between them. She could feel Kelly's wetness. "I want to make you feel as good as you just made me feel." She pressed her hips down, increasing the contact between them.

Kelly let out a gasp as Logan rubbed against her. It spurred Logan on. She increased the speed and pressure until Kelly's arms tightened around her and an orgasm ripped through her.

"Now I'm happy," Logan said. "You?"

"Can't...talk...yet."

"Those sounded like words to me." She nuzzled her face into Kelly's neck and breathed in the essence of her. She would be content to stay like this forever.

CHAPTER FIFTEEN

"What did Rachel say about us being together?" Logan asked as Kelly spooned scrambled eggs onto her plate. It was a nice change spending the night at Kelly's and helping her make breakfast in the morning.

She'd updated Olivia and even told her mother about Kelly. Both Olivia and her mom were anxious to meet her.

"That was kind of a random question." Kelly put the frying pan back on the stove.

"I'm kind of a random person. I talked to my sister about us. She was very happy for me."

"I haven't told Rachel yet."

Logan stopped pouring orange juice, mid-stream. "What? Why not? We've been together for…" she stopped to think. "Over three weeks now. I thought for sure you would have told her."

Kelly shrugged.

"That is not an answer." Rachel seemed so concerned about the possibility of them being together or Logan hurting Kelly, Logan wanted to know how she felt now. She wondered if Kelly not telling her was cause for concern.

"I guess I wanted to keep this close to the vest for a while. Keep it all for myself if that makes sense."

Logan put a plate of bacon on the table and settled down in a chair across from Kelly. "Do you think she would disapprove?"

Kelly seemed to think about it for a few moments. "No. It's not that." She scrunched up her face.

"What aren't you telling me?"

Kelly snatched a piece of bacon from the plate. She hesitated before answering. "I wanted to make sure this was real."

"This is as real as it gets. At least for me. I hope you feel the same way," Logan said.

"I do. It's just that my past has proven to be a series of relationships that weren't real, starting with my mother and more recently Paula."

Logan could understand her reluctance to share anything so soon. "I'm not them," she said.

Kelly placed her hand on top of Logan's. "I know that. But I'm still me and I have some baggage that I'm still trying to unpack. It's not that I want to hide this. I'm so proud to be with you."

"I do understand. Hand me one of those suitcases and I'll help empty it." She would do anything to help with that.

"You've already unpacked more than you know. And I so appreciate it. The pile is getting smaller all the time."

"I'm willing to keep working on it with you until it's gone."

Kelly smiled. "You know it will never be all the way gone. Right?"

"I do. I guess we will just have to work on it forever. Together." Logan hoped that talking about a future so soon didn't scare Kelly off. Judging by the smile on her face, Logan figured it was a safe thing to say. She'd never talked about a future together with someone this early before. Things felt different with Kelly. Safer.

"Not to beat a dead horse," Logan said. "But *do* you plan on telling Rachel?"

"You beat dead horses?"

"I said *not* to beat one."

"Oh. Okay. I don't approve of beating any animals. Alive or dead. And yes. I plan on telling Rachel, very soon."

"Does that mean you are starting to feel more secure with me?"

Kelly nodded. "I'm sorry if you think I've been dragging my feet."

"I didn't think that. And don't apologize for your feelings. Your skepticism is understandable. I'll do whatever it takes to prove to you that I am not like those other people."

"You already have."

"I'm glad. Now eat your breakfast. You have dogs to walk in a little while."

"What are your plans for the day?" Kelly bit into a piece of toast.

"Work at three. Filling in for Helen today. Before that, not much. Maybe go hang with my mom for a bit."

"I miss you already and you haven't even left yet."

"You know where to find me if you want to come by the bar later."

"I may see if Rachel is free tonight."

"Bring her by."

Kelly laughed. "Yeah. No. I want to tell her about us, but it would feel weird with you a few feet away."

"You don't have to do that just because I asked. Do it when you're ready."

"I am ready. Today seems like the perfect time. You asking just reminded me. That's all. Okay?"

"Of course. Give Rachel my best."

"Don't be giving your best away. You should save that for me." Kelly smiled.

That smile reminded Logan of why she was so crazy about her. "You got my best, sweetie. Give Rachel my mediocre."

"You are so accommodating."

"It's my best feature."

❖

Kelly called Rachel in between jobs, and they agreed to meet at Kelly's apartment when Rachel was done with work. The day seemed to drag until Kelly gave her last dog for the day his treat and headed home. She had about an hour before Rachel was expected and she spent the time cutting cheese, layering them on a plate with crackers and preparing other snacks and drinks.

She was finished by the time Rachel knocked on her door.

"Hey there," Rachel said. "I haven't seen you in a while. I'm glad you called."

"I know. Sorry about that. Come on in. I have snacks."

"Snacks." Rachel said "Why didn't you tell me that on the phone. I would have been here sooner." She held up a bottle. "I have the wine."

"My kind of woman." Kelly set the plate of food down on the table and took two wine glasses down from the cabinet.

"I thought Logan was your kind of woman."

"She doesn't drink wine."

"Sorry. Guess it's not a match made in heaven after all."

Rachel searched the utensil draw for the corkscrew and came up empty.

"It's on the counter," Kelly said. "Speaking of Logan and matches and heaven," Kelly started.

Rachel opened the wine and poured out two glasses. "What about Logan?"

"Let's sit," Kelly said.

"Sounds serious." Rachel handed a glass of wine to Kelly, set the bottle on the table, and sat.

Kelly sat across from her. "It is serious. At least I hope it gets serious." She took a large sip of her wine. Guess this is why they call it liquid courage.

"Care to tell me what we're talking about? You okay?"

"Rachel, I'm more than okay."

"I think I need a little more information." Rachel grabbed a cracker and placed a piece of cheese on top.

"Logan and I are—" Kelly paused. "Together." Kelly watched Rachel, waiting for her reaction.

Rachel had the food halfway to her mouth and stopped. "What does together mean?" Rachel's face lit up as the realization hit her. "Oh. You mean together together. Oh, Kelly. When? How? I'm so happy for you. Are you happy? Who started it? I knew you had feelings and I told you Logan was looking at you different than she was looking at everyone else. I hate to say I told you so…but. Are you going to fill me in or leave me hanging?"

Kelly waited for Rachel to take a breath. "Want me to answer now or do you have a dozen more questions?" She chuckled.

"I have a ton more questions, but you can answer those first."

"Start over. One question at a time."

"When?"

Kelly swallowed hard. "Umm. Logan told me about her feelings the night she invited me to the bar. The night I asked you if you wanted to go and you said you couldn't."

It seemed like it took several seconds for Rachel to remember when that was. "That was weeks ago. How come you didn't tell me this before now?"

That was the question Kelly wasn't sure how to answer to Rachel's satisfaction. "I wanted to make sure it was real."

"To make sure she wasn't using you?"

Kelly shook her head. "No. I didn't think that. But I…" She hesitated. "I don't know. I wanted to make sure she really liked me and wasn't going to change her mind."

"Why would she change her mind?"

"You know my history. It wouldn't be the first time." Kelly took another sip of her wine.

Rachel nodded. "Stupid people." She put the cheese and cracker in her mouth and wiped her hands on a napkin.

"She kissed me, Rachel. She kissed me that day, like I've never been kissed before. At least it caused feelings in me like I've never felt before."

"She kissed you in the bar? In front of everyone?"

Kelly laughed. "No. In her apartment, on her break. Oh, and then again in the back room at the bar. It was heaven, Rachel."

"I can only imagine. Who would have thought it? Ms. Hottie and Kelly." She whistled.

"Stop. She's more than hot. She is hot. So hot. But she's so much more, Rachel. She's kind and caring and…and…and just so wonderful."

"You really like her, don't you?"

"It's so much more than that." She finished the wine in her glass and poured another.

"Was there more than two kisses? I mean have you actually gone out on a date? I mean you must have. Weeks, Kelly. It's been weeks. Tell me."

Kelly filled Rachel in. She left out the fact that they were also sleeping together.

"If you're happy, I'm happy." Rachel said. "And I can tell you're happy. If she does anything to hurt you, she is going to be one sorry bartender."

"Please don't be like that. I appreciate your looking out for me, but I want you to be on board with this."

Rachel patted Kelly's hand. "Oh, honey, I am. I only want the best for you. When are you going to see her again?"

"It's a little tricky with our schedules. I can always go to the bar and hang out…with a roomful of other people. Not exactly the most romantic way to spend our time."

"I'll go with you if you want. We haven't gone out in forever. We can chat and you can ogle your girlfriend."

Kelly laughed. "That might be a good plan. Maybe tomorrow night? Although it's Friday and it'll be packed."

"We can go tonight if you want. Logan's on duty, isn't she?"

"She is. But she just left here this morning. I don't want to seem desperate."

"This morning? For breakfast or for the end of a sleepover?"

Oh shit. Didn't mean to say that. "Both."

"Both? I think you left this part out earlier."

"Okay. Yeah. We've slept together."

"Was last night the first time?"

"No." Kelly's face warmed and she could tell she was blushing.

"And?"

"And what?" There was no way, as close as she was to Rachel, that she was going to share actual details.

"Is it good?"

"Good? Is it good?" Kelly tried not to smirk.

"That's the question."

"It's beyond spectacular. And that's all the details you're getting."

"That's all the details I want."

"Really?"

"No. But I'll have to sneak the questions in when your guard is down."

"Sounds like something you would do."

Rachel put her hand under her chin and batted her eyelashes. "You know me so well." She popped another cheese and cracker in her mouth.

❖

Logan was surprised and caught a little off guard when she saw Rachel walk into the bar. Kelly had texted her the night before to let her know she'd told Rachel about them, and it went well. She wondered if Rachel was there to reprimand her or give her a piece of her mind. Not that Logan was scared of her, but she wanted Kelly's friends to like her—and trust her. Logan finished ringing up a drink order, handed the credit card and receipt to the customer, and went to the end of the bar where Rachel had settled herself down. "Hi, Rachel. How are you doing? What can I get you?" She readied herself for an attack.

"The usual please. Kelly should be here in about ten minutes. I wanted to talk to you first."

Logan grabbed a glass from under the bar. "Everything okay? Kelly didn't mention that the two of you were coming by tonight."

"She told me what's going on with you two. I'm happy for her. Please take care of her heart." It was no attack. It was someone trying to protect her friend.

"Her heart is very important to me. This is for real. I'm not a game player and the last person I would ever *play* with, if I was, is Kelly. So, you really don't have anything to worry about."

"Good to know. I'll take you at your word."

Logan finished making Rachel's drink and set it down in front of her. "We both want what's best for her," she said.

"Speak of the devil," Rachel said, raising her drink in the direction of the door.

Logan's heart did that little flip-floppy thing at the sight of Kelly.

"Who are you calling a devil?" Kelly asked Rachel.

"You heard that? Holy shit. Do you have supersonic hearing?"

Kelly ignored the question. She turned to Logan. "Hi," she said almost shyly.

"Hi. This is a nice surprise. I'm happy to see you."

"Me too."

"More *me toos*?" Logan asked.

Kelly laughed. "That was the last one."

From the corner of her eye, Logan could see Rachel looking from Kelly to her with a confused look on her face. She was too interested in talking to Kelly to try to explain. Kelly obviously hadn't noticed.

Logan leaned her forearms on the bar and leaned close to Kelly. "I want to kiss you," she whispered.

"Me…I mean…I would like that very much."

"You're being paged." Rachel pointed to a woman seated several seats over.

Logan turned her head in that direction and held up one finger. She turned back to Kelly. "Water? Soda?" She raised her eyebrows. "Something with alcohol?"

"Let me think about it while you see what that customer wants. That way I get to watch you walk away and I can look forward to you coming back."

Logan couldn't help but smile. She gave a small salute and went to wait on the customer.

"I've never seen you act this way with anyone before," Rachel said to Kelly.

"Like what?" Kelly turned to her, tearing her eyes away from Logan with difficulty.

"Bold. Confident. Flirty."

Kelly knew she felt different with Logan. She didn't realize she was acting different as well. "Is that a bad thing?"

Rachel shook her head. "No. Not at all. I love it. It's about time you grew a pair and had confidence in yourself. If that's because of Logan, I'll have to thank her."

"So much of it is due to her. She won't let me put myself down and she believes in me."

Rachel swatted her on the arm. "Geez. I've been trying to do that for years."

"Hey." Kelly rubbed her arm, exaggerating her reaction. "I guess it took one more person telling me those things in order to absorb it. Sorry I didn't listen to you."

"I'll forgive you as long as you don't forget the lesson."

"Are you hitting my girlfriend?" Kelly didn't realize that Logan had returned.

"It's just a flesh wound," Kelly said. Girlfriend. The word didn't escape Kelly's notice.

"I barely touched her." Rachel raised both her hands in front of her.

"It's okay. I'll heal. In a week or two. But I may need someone to kiss me and make me feel better."

"What are you, twelve?" Rachel asked.

"Hey. If you had someone like Logan, you would take any kisses you could get."

Logan took her hand. "You don't need an excuse for me to kiss you, you know." She leaned in closer. "Anywhere. Anytime."

The thought made Kelly's stomach clench.

"Did you decide what you want to drink?"

"Let's live dangerously. Sloe gin fizz. Please. Rachel's treat."

"You got it, honey. Be right back."

"You're positively giddy. And more than a little silly around Logan," Rachel said.

"Am I being stupid?" Kelly asked her.

"Not at all. It's cute."

Logan returned with Kelly's drink. "Sunday. Get together?"

Kelly hoped they could spend Logan's next day off together, but she didn't want to push. "Absolutely."

"Good. Busy night. I'll stop over when I can, or flag me over if you two need refills." Logan leaned over the bar and kissed Kelly on the cheek.

The sensation of Logan's lips left a warm spot on Kelly's heart and a wet spot somewhere else.

"Guess you won't get to spend too much time with Logan tonight. Sorry."

"Hey. We knew that it would be busy. Besides, I'm here to spend time with you too. How is your life going?"

"Same old. Same old. Nothing new. Mark got that promotion he was after."

"That's great."

"Yes and no. More money coming in is. Mark spending more time at work isn't."

They spent the rest of the evening talking mostly about Rachel's life with Logan popping over whenever she could.

Rachel paid their tab, hugged Kelly, and said her good-byes. Kelly was gearing up to leave too. She wanted to wait until Logan had a chance to come back over so she could say good-bye. She didn't have long to wait.

"Why don't I give you my key and you can go upstairs? I don't get off till two, but I would love to have you in my bed when I go home." She put up her hands. "No pressure. But if it would help, I will be really quiet and not wake you up."

"And what if I said I want you to make a lot of noise when you come up and *accidently* wake me up?" She wanted to be awake when Logan slipped into bed next to her. She knew Logan may be too tired to make love after such a busy night and she was okay with that. Just to lie next to her in bed while they slept would be amazing.

"That can be arranged." She pulled a key from her pocket and handed it to Kelly. "Slip it under the welcome mat after you go in. That way you can lock the door and I can still get in. There are T-shirts in the top drawer of my dresser if you want something to slip on."

"And I want to do that why? Wouldn't I be more comfortable without any clothes on?"

"I want you to be comfortable, so do whatever you need to do."

Kelly looked into Logan's deep green eyes and wished she could kiss her. Patience, she thought. I'll kiss the hell out of her when she's off work.

"I'll see you soon," Kelly gave Logan her best smile. She headed out the front door, drove her car around the back, and made her way up the stairs to Logan's apartment. She felt a little weird letting herself in when Logan wasn't home, but it wasn't like she hadn't already spent several nights in Logan's apartment.

She had just slipped the key under the welcome mat when her phone pinged with a text. It was from Logan. *There is a new toothbrush on the counter in the master bath for you.*

Logan was full of surprises. Kelly had never been so happy with a gift and the thoughtfulness behind it. *You are the best,* Kelly texted back. She added three hearts, then deleted them. Too soon.

I know. I'll see you later.

Kelly got herself ready for bed and slipped under the covers. Bear jumped up and made himself comfortable next to her. "Hey, little man."

He purred his reply.

Kelly closed her eyes, but sleep refused to cooperate. The anticipation of Logan, naked, next to her, overtook her brain and most of her senses. Watching YouTube videos on her phone seemed to be a short-term solution. She was still awake when she heard the door open and close. Bear jumped off the bed and Kelly assumed he went to greet Logan.

Kelly turned off her phone, set it on the nightstand, rolled onto her side, and closed her eyes. She pretended to be asleep when she heard Logan tiptoe in, go into the bathroom and close the door with barely a click.

Logan slipped into bed a few minutes later, cuddled up to Kelly's back and wrapped an arm around her.

Kelly waited for several long seconds before quickly turning in Logan's arms to face her. "Hi," she said. "Where ya been? At the bar again? How are we ever going to make this work if you're at the bar all night?"

"Oh my God. I thought you were asleep. You startled me." She placed a kiss on Kelly's nose.

"Hi," Kelly said again.

"Hi yourself. How come you aren't sleeping?"

"How come you didn't make a lot of noise like I asked you to?"

"Silly woman. I figured you would need your sleep, so you had extra strength for the morning, when I make mad passionate love to you." She planted several kisses along Kelly's jawline and worked her way over to Kelly's mouth.

Kelly knew she wouldn't have to wait till morning.

CHAPTER SIXTEEN

K elly woke up content with Logan's arms wrapped around her. She snuggled in closer and couldn't help placing small kisses along Logan's shoulder and neck.

"Mmm," Logan said. "Good morning."

"Should I let you sleep? You worked until pretty late. And then...well, you didn't exactly go right to sleep when you got home."

"You were awake as long as I was. Do you need more sleep?"

"Not when I'm this close to you. Perhaps a shower would help you wake up. We can take a nap later if you want."

"We both know that we wouldn't get much sleep if we lay down in bed together in the middle of the day." Logan let out a long yawn.

"Then I think I should nap on the couch...with you lying on top of me. Do you think we could sleep then?"

Logan gave a halfhearted attempt at sitting but gave up. "Kelly?"

"Yes."

"Remember how I said we should take it slow?"

Kelly's stomach did an uncomfortable flip. *Slow* didn't last long before they dived in headfirst. Kelly was afraid Logan wanted to pull back. "Yes."

"Obviously, we haven't been taking it slow. I mean, we have by lesbian standards. We didn't move in together on the second date." She laughed.

Kelly nodded, still not sure where Logan was going with this.

"I'm very happy with where we are. I'm glad we didn't go any slower."

Kelly let out a sigh of relief. "I feel the same."

"I just felt you stiffen up and then relax. Did you think I was going to say something else?"

Kelly closed her eyes against the tears that welled up. She wasn't sure if it was from the initial fear or the relief she felt. She nodded.

"Kelly, look at me."

A few tears spilled out of her eyes when she opened them.

Logan brushed them away. "I'm all in. I'm not going anywhere. How can I get you to relax?"

"Just telling me that helps. A lot."

"I know you've had bad relationships in the past. But that's not what this is."

"I know. I'll do better."

"You don't need to do better. Just trust me. That's all I ask."

"I do." That was all Kelly had a chance to say before Logan claimed her mouth with her own. All thoughts went out of Kelly's head as the sensations in her body took over.

❖

"Are you working today?" Logan asked Kelly over a late breakfast.

"I am not. But you are, aren't you?"

"Yeah, I'm scheduled for four but can probably push it back to five. Thought maybe we could go do something."

Kelly smiled. "Of course. What did you have in mind?" The more time she got to spend with Logan the better.

"Have you ever kayaked?"

"No. You should know I'm not the most coordinated person. I'm not sure how good I would be at it." The last thing she wanted to do was make a fool out of herself in front of Logan. Of course, if anyone would be okay with her looking like a fool it would be Logan.

"It's easy. I'll help you get started. I know where we can go. They rent kayaks and it's an easy spot to get them into the water. I've been at places where you have to practically jump in the kayak from the dock."

"I would like to see you do that," Kelly said with a laugh.

"It's not a pretty sight."

"I can't image anything involving you that wouldn't be pretty."

Logan finished loading the breakfast dishes into the dishwasher and they were on their way. It was a short drive to the water. Kelly was still a little anxious, but trusted Logan would help her.

Logan took care of the rentals and helped Kelly put on her life vest. They made their way to the water to where the kayaks were lined up. "You can pick any one you want," Logan said. "How about that orange one? That color would go great with your eyes." She smiled.

"That's how you choose?" Kelly asked. "By color-coordinating?"

"Of course. How else?"

"Good a plan as any."

"Oh. Almost forgot." Logan pulled a small tube of sunscreen from her pants pocket and tossed it to Kelly. "Got to protect that gorgeous skin of yours."

Kelly squirted a small amount in her hand and proceeded to rub it on her arms, legs, and face. "I've been told my skin is nice enough to kill me for."

"Say what?"

Kelly laughed. "Nothing. Just a bad joke."

"Someone wants to kill you for your skin? I could understand killing you for your kidney, but not skin. I mean, what would they even do with it?"

"Damn if I know. I would prefer not to be killed for my body parts at all." Kelly tossed the tube back to Logan.

"I get it." Logan applied the sunscreen and pocketed the tube.

They each pulled their kayak to the water's edge. Logan helped Kelly into hers and gave it a shove to get it fully into the water. Made it through that part without falling in the water, Kelly thought. So far, so good. She hoped she could keep up with Logan when they started moving.

Logan was only seconds behind her. "How ya doing?"

"Good."

Logan demonstrated how to use the paddles correctly.

Kelly followed Logan's lead and to her amazement the kayak moved forward. "It works."

Logan laughed. "See. It's not hard. You got this."

"Holy cow. I do. This is fun."

"You like?" Logan paddled in a circle around Kelly.

"Now, you're just showing off." Kelly laughed.

"I'm trying to impress my woman. Are you impressed?"

My woman? Kelly liked that. Liked it a lot. "I am *so* impressed." And so crazy about you.

"Left or right?"

"What?"

"Should we go to the left or to the right?"

Kelly looked both ways. The left was lined with trees, while the right was more open. She'd always liked being in the woods as a kid. It was quiet. Peaceful. There were few places that did that for her when she was young. "Left."

"You got it. Use the left side of the paddle and it will turn you in the right direction."

"I'll go right if I paddle left?"

Logan laughed. "No. If you paddle left it will be *correct.*"

"Okay. Got it." Kelly was able to maneuver the kayak in the correct direction. It wasn't nearly as hard as she thought it would be.

Sunlight filtered through the trees and bounced off the water in silver and gold rippling slivers. It was a beautiful day for a ride down the river with the woman she cared so much about.

They slowed down to let a mama duck, followed closely by her five ducklings, cross in front of them. "That's a mallard and her babies," Kelly said.

"I thought they had green heads."

"The males do. The females are brown like that." As if on cue, the mother duck turned and let out a series of quacks. "She does that to make sure the babies are following her."

"Where's the daddy duck?"

"He usually hangs around until the eggs hatch and then he's off partying with the other guys."

"Jerk."

They paddled on in silence for several minutes.

"I love the water," Logan said.

"Do you ever go fishing?"

"I did when I was younger. My father was big into it. My mother and sister, not so much. So, it would just be him and me. My mother would pack us a lunch and off to the lake we would go."

"Did you have a boat?"

"No. We would cast from the shore. When I got older, I stopped fishing but would sometimes go with him, just to be with him. You know?"

Kelly didn't. No father and no desire to just *be* with her mother. Ever. She really didn't know what that was like. "How come you stopped fishing?"

"It just seemed cruel. I never shared my thoughts with my dad. I didn't want to take away what he loved so much."

"Cruel? You mean to use worms?"

Logan seemed to think about it for a few seconds. "Yeah. Not fun for the worm, but not kind to the fish either. I mean, there you are, swimming around the lake, not a care in the world. You see a tasty tidbit in front of you, casually saunter over to it to take a nibble, and suddenly you are being dragged around by your lips, fighting for your life."

"What about catch and release? Did that seem cruel as well?"

"Yes. Think of the therapy bills that poor fish must have racked up once he was back in the water. It's like when people get abducted by aliens. First of all, no one believes them, and it takes years for them to get over the experience, if they ever really do."

"You believe in alien abductions?" Kelly asked, surprised.

"Of course not. I don't believe anyone that says that. Just like the other fish don't believe their buddy was abducted by humans."

Kelly laughed. She seemed to be doing that a lot more lately. "You're crazy."

"I know. Some say it's my best feature."

"You seem to have an awful lot of those. Best features, I mean."

"I do. I'm glad you finally noticed."

"I noticed your best features right from the start. You do have a lot of them."

"I know. It's a burden sometimes, but one I'm forced to live with."

Kelly tried to bring her paddle up quickly in Logan's direction, but her paddle failed to cooperate, and she couldn't splash Logan like she'd planned.

"Is this what you're trying to do?" Logan asked, splashing water in Kelly's direction, and drenching her arm in the process.

"Hey."

"What?"

"You got me all wet," Kelly said.

"I like it when you're wet."

Kelly sucked in a breath. God. How could someone turn her on in a split second with a joke. Granted it was a sexual joke, but geez.

"No response," Logan said after several seconds.

"I'm thinking."

"Of a response?"

Kelly shook her head. "No, of you making me wet." She couldn't believe she'd just said that. Rachel had been right. She'd never been this bold with anyone before. But Logan somehow made her brave enough to do it.

"Ooh. Damn. Now you've got me thinking about it. How am I going to make it through the rest of the day with these thoughts running through my head?"

"I don't know. Anything I can do to help?"

"I wish. I'm afraid we won't have time for you to help. I'll just have to suffer in silence."

"Thinking about me makes you suffer?"

"No. Thinking about you makes me happy. Thinking about touching you and not being able to makes me suffer."

"I can understand that. Let's talk about something else. Try to get your mind off it. Umm. Let's see, we talked about ducks, fishing, alien abductions. I'm not sure there's anything left to talk about."

"There must be something."

"Nope. We've covered it all."

"Well, damn."

They watched in silence as a raccoon helped himself to a drink at the edge of the water.

"That's so cool," Kelly whispered when he disappeared back into the woods.

Logan agreed.

Kelly closed her eyes and let herself drift for a bit as birds serenaded them from high above in the trees. Peace. That was the word for it. Floating on a river of peace. That was how she felt anytime she was around Logan. The water just magnified the feeling.

"Doing okay?" Logan asked.

Kelly blinked her eyes open. She didn't realize that Logan had come up so close beside her. "Yes. Just enjoying the…the everything. I'm enjoying everything. Especially the company."

"Ditto. I'm glad you are adventurous enough to try something new with me."

Kelly set her kayak in motion once more. "I would try anything you want me to do."

It only took a couple seconds for Logan to catch up to her. "Anything?" She wiggled her eyebrows.

Kelly thought about it for a moment. "I totally trust you. Anything."

Logan's smile spread across her face. "Good to know." She paddled ahead of Kelly and turned her kayak around. "Hate to say it, but we need to head back so I can get ready for work."

"Aww. I'd stamp my foot, but I can't quite maneuver that right now." She reluctantly turned her kayak around.

"I cleaned out a drawer in the dresser and some space in the closet for you," Logan said to Kelly on the drive back.

First a toothbrush and now this. "No one's ever done that for me before. I'm truly touched."

Logan reached for her hand. "Then it's about time. A girl's got to have a place to keep her clean underwear when she sleeps over. Which I hope is often." She gave Kelly's hand a squeeze.

"I can't believe how good you are to me," Kelly said. "I don't deserve…" She let the words drift off.

"You were going to say you don't deserve it, weren't you?"

"I was. But stopped."

"Did you stop because you realized you were wrong or because you knew I would object?"

Kelly thought about it for a second. "Both, I guess. I really haven't *done* anything to deserve it, but you like me so that is a good enough reason for you to be good to me." Kelly shook her head. "I'm not sure that made sense."

"It makes perfect sense. And I do like you. I really, really like you. And you *do* deserve to be treated good. And not *just* because I like you." She looked over at Kelly for a second. "Kelly, you are more than worthy to be treated well and cared for just because you're you."

"All right."

"Let that sink in."

"I will."

"Do you mind if we make a quick pit stop?"

"Not at all. Where?"

"My mom's house. You okay with that? Be honest."

Kelly didn't mind meeting new people. But this wasn't just people. This was Logan's mother. She looked down at her clothes, jean shorts and a T-shirt. She wasn't going to make a very good impression.

"Stop," Logan said, as if reading her mind. "You look great. My mother isn't going to care what you're wearing. And we won't stay long. If you don't want to go, all you have to do is tell me."

"It's fine. You don't think it's too soon? Wait. I thought you had to go to work."

"It would be too soon if I had doubts about my feelings for you. I don't. And as far as work goes, I've still got some time before I need to be there. So? What do you think? Are you up for it? I can drop you off at home after. She doesn't live far from you."

Kelly swallowed down the nerves that seemed to appear out of nowhere. "Sure."

Logan rested her hand on top of Kelly's and gave it a squeeze.

"You sure I look okay?" Kelly asked as they approached the house.

"Yes. Of course. I'm dressed pretty much the same way you are."

"Yeah, but you've already met your mother. This is my first time."

Logan laughed and took her hand. "You look great. She's going to love you. I promise."

Kelly was surprised when someone about her age opened the door. Either Logan's mother looked extremely young for her age, or this wasn't her mother.

"Olivia," Logan said. "What are you doing here?"

"Hope it's all right. Mom said you might stop over, and I wanted to meet the famous Kelly." Olivia offered her hand. "Hi. I'm Olivia, Logan's sister."

"Nice to meet you." Kelly dropped Logan's hand only long enough to shake Olivia's and then grabbed it again. She hoped no one else had dropped by to meet her. At least not today.

"Logan has said such nice things about you."

Kelly glanced up at Logan. "She has?"

"I have. And if Olivia would let us in, I might say nice things about her too." Logan smiled.

"Oh sure. Sorry." She stepped back. "Mom is on the patio in the back yard."

Kelly held on tight to Logan's hand as they made their way through the house, followed by Olivia.

Logan's mother stood up as soon as they passed through the sliding glass doors that led outside. She took Kelly's hand in her own. "You must be Kelly," she said. "It's so nice to meet you. Come. Sit. You too, Logan."

"Thank you, Mrs. Spencer. It's very nice to meet you as well."

"Call me Barbara," she said. "Olivia, could you get a couple more glasses of iced tea please?"

Logan led Kelly over to a wicker love seat across from her mother. The cushions looked old and crinkled when they sat down, but it was surprisingly comfortable.

"We can't stay long, Mom. I have to bring Kelly home soon and go to work."

"You have a lovely yard, Mrs. Spenc—Barbara," Kelly said. The lawn was neatly trimmed and several rose bushes in full bloom lined the back fence. Two very tall oak trees stood at attention in opposite corners, offering some much needed shade. A small glass table sat on one side of the patio surrounded by four matching chairs. Logan's mom sat in a wooden rocker that looked like it was at least fifty years old.

"Thank you. Logan helps out with the lawn. I don't know what I would do without her."

Kelly squeezed Logan's hand.

"I'm so glad you could stop over. Logan said you're a dog walker. I think that's so great. Do you like it?"

"I do. I love animals. Unfortunately, I'm not allowed to have a dog where I live."

"That's too bad. And I know you're the one who gave Bear to Logan. That was so kind of you. I know Logan loves him a lot."

"He's a good cat," Kelly said. Talking to Logan's mother wasn't nearly as hard as she thought it would be. Logan came from *good people* she thought, using the term Logan had used for her.

Oliva returned with two glasses of iced tea and handed Logan and Kelly each one. "Need a refill, Mom?" she asked.

Barbara held up her half full glass. "All set, honey. Thanks."

Olivia pulled one of the patio chairs closer to the group and sat. "What did you two do today? You look like you got some sun."

"Kayaking," Kelly said. "It was my first time."

"She did great," Logan added. "Picked it up like a pro."

"I had a good teacher," Kelly said.

"Did you like it?" Barbara asked.

"I did. I was nervous at first. I'm not the most coordinated person and thought for sure I would end up in the water."

"You have plenty of coordination," Logan said. "Didn't you tell me that you sometimes walk four dogs at once? That takes coordination."

Kelly didn't mean to put herself down. Some habits were hard to break. "I do," she said. "Once in a while." She turned to Logan's mom and continued. "One of my clients has two dogs and when her son visits, he brings his two."

"What kind of dogs are they?" Olivia asked.

"Two very large German shepherds and two little schnoodles."

"What's a schnoodle? Sounds more like a dessert than a dog," Logan's mother said.

Kelly laughed. She liked her. "It's a cross between a poodle and a schnauzer."

"In my day we called those mutts," Barbara said with a giggle.

"They call them designer dogs now," Logan added.

Kelly looked at her. "That's right. How did you know that?"

"I have brains," Logan said. "Some say it's my—"

"Best feature," both Olivia and Barbara said, before Logan had a chance to finish her sentence.

Kelly laughed. Yes, she liked Logan's mom, and her sister too.

❖

"That wasn't so bad, was it?" Logan asked as they drove to Kelly's apartment.

"No. Not at all. I like them. They seem very kind and caring. I can see why you are so great."

"They are pretty good, aren't they? I'm very lucky." Logan paused. "I'm sorry. That was very insensitive of me."

"What are you talking about?"

"Me saying I'm lucky, when you had such a rough childhood and no real family."

"You are lucky, and you're allowed to say it. My childhood only makes me appreciate you and your family more."

"I just don't ever want to make you feel bad. About anything," Logan said.

"You don't. You don't need to watch every word you say to me. I'm going to tell you what you told me. I just want you to be you. That's all I ask."

"That's all you ask? Nothing more? There's nothing more you want from me?"

Kelly thought about it for several moments. "That and your kisses and caresses and your naked body next to me and on top of me." She paused. "Should I go on?"

"I'm not sure I'm going to make it to work if you do. You've got a way with words. You know that? I am very turned on at the moment. I'm glad you didn't say this stuff at my mother's."

"She gave me her number. Your sister did too. I can always text it to them if you think it will help us get closer."

Logan laughed. "And you say I'm the goof."

"I do say you're the goof. It's one of your best features," Kelly said and laughed.

❖

At Logan's insistence, Kelly had brought over several outfits, underwear, and even a teddy that she hoped Logan would like.

"There's another trivia contest at that bar," Logan said as they were loading the dishwasher after lunch. "We should go and defend our title."

"Are you just using me for my brain?" Kelly stacked the plates on the bottom rack.

Logan pulled her up and into her arms. "Yes. Your brain, your body, your heart. Especially your body." She kissed Kelly full on the mouth.

"I can live with that."

They finished cleaning up and Kelly sat next to Logan on the couch. "Can I ask you to do me a favor?" Logan asked.

"Of course. Anything."

Logan bit her bottom lip. "Would you mind sitting across from me?" Logan pointed across the room. "In that chair?"

Kelly was confused. "You don't want me to sit next to you?"

"I love when we sit close. But I started a drawing a while ago." Logan pulled her sketch book and a few pencils from the drawer in the coffee table and showed it to Kelly.

She recognized Bear right away but was confused by the woman figure. "That's really good," Kelly said.

"It's you and Bear," Logan said. "But see I didn't draw your face. If you can sit in that chair...see, I drew the chair...I can finish it. I didn't think I could do justice to your beautiful face unless you were in front of me."

Kelly attempted to finger comb her hair.

Logan took her hand. "Stop. I love your hair with a piece or two out of place."

"There's probably more than that out of place. It's probably a mess."

Logan kissed her. "It's not a mess. And I love you just the way you are."

Love? Kelly had been tossing that word around in her own mind for weeks but didn't have enough courage to be the first one to say it. But Logan said it. Did she mean it?

"Kelly?"

"Umm."

"Kelly, I do. I love you."

"I love you too."

"You don't have to say that just because I did," Logan said.

Kelly pulled her into a tight hug. "I do love you. So much." And Logan loved her back. Her life had never been so good. Ever.

Logan pulled back enough to look into Kelly's eyes. "Are you happy?"

"Extremely." That word didn't seem nearly adequate.

"Good. I would hate to be this happy alone."

Kelly reluctantly let Logan go and sat across from her in the chair.

"Cross your legs and turn your whole body a little to the left," Logan said. "I'll be able to add more details to your body if you're in the same position that I originally drew you in."

"Would it help if Bear was sitting on my lap?"

Logan pointed at her with a drawing pencil. "You know that's a great idea. Don't move. I'll go find him."

Logan returned with Bear in her arms and deposited the large orange cat on Kelly's lap. He settled right down as if he belonged there.

Logan set about drawing them. Kelly couldn't see what she was doing, but she seemed to be lost in the process. Her level of concentration was amazing.

"Sorry, that took so long," she said at last. "Want to see it?"

"Of course."

"Come on over."

Kelly set Bear down on the chair and took a seat next to Logan. The drawing was incredible. Kelly had no idea Logan was that talented. "You made me look so much better than I actually do."

"No, Kelly. You are that beautiful. You've come a long way, but you still don't believe that do you?"

Kelly shrugged. "I believe you believe it."

"Look at the drawing again, Kelly. Can you agree that you look beautiful in this drawing?"

Kelly had to agree that she did.

"This is what you really look like. Not just to me. To the world, Kelly. You *are* this beautiful."

"Thank you."

"You don't have to thank me for telling the truth. I'm glad I got a chance to finish the drawing."

"You completed me." Kelly smiled.

"*You* already were complete."

"I don't know. I seem to have had missing parts for a long time."

"We all have bits and pieces scattered here and there. But that's what life's all about. Gathering our pieces and sticking them back in. Sometimes they're perfect. Sometimes they're a little wonky. But we should still claim and welcome them all."

"That was beautifully said."

"I am in love with all your parts, Kelly."

"Even the wonky ones?"

"Especially the wonky ones," Logan said.

Kelly didn't think she could have loved Logan any more than she did. She was wrong.

EPILOGUE

L ogan unpacked the last box, adding her books to Kelly's already on the bookshelf. Moving wasn't her favorite thing to do, but it was worth all the hard work to be able to share a house with Kelly.

"Hey there. How did it go?" Logan asked when Kelly walked in. "It looks like it's starting to rain."

"Our first walk around the block was a massive success. He peed and pooped. And it is starting to sprinkle out there."

Logan knelt in front of the mutt, scratched his ears, and roughed up the white fur around his neck, a complete contrast to the midnight black on the rest of his body. "What a good boy you are. Yes. You are." She unhooked the leash, and he ran off, probably in search of Bear. Logan was so glad there was no sibling rivalry. They were on their way to becoming best friends.

Kelly offered a hand and pulled Logan to her feet. Logan wrapped her arms around Kelly and snuggled into her, placing small kisses along her neck.

"Have I told you lately how much I love you," Logan asked. "And how I can't wait to make you my wife?"

"You told me this morning, but you can tell me again."

"Two weeks. Two weeks and we will be walking down that aisle." She rocked Kelly side to side. "I got the last box unpacked. We are officially all moved in."

"You have done a great job, honey."

"*We* have done a great job. You did as much as I did. Although you didn't do much yesterday and today except play with the dog." She laughed.

"Just trying to let Tupper know that he is an important part of the family. Are you feeling left out?"

"No. I get to hug you in the living room like this and sleep with you at night. Tupper only gets to go on walks with you."

"You're the one who said Tupper can't sleep in the bed."

"He weighs fifty pounds. He would interfere with our sleeping. Not to mention our cuddling and other things. It's bad enough Bear tries to sleep on my head."

"You love it."

"Okay. I do. But I love you more."

"I love you too."

The house and even the dog had been Logan's idea. She still had the ability to surprise and thrill Kelly, even after a year together. And happiness didn't even adequately describe how Kelly felt.

The house wasn't huge, but it was big enough for the two of them and their two fur babies. And no stairs meant Logan's mom could visit. Kelly had come to think of her as family. She treated Kelly like a daughter. Through Logan she finally got the mother she always wanted, and a sister as well. Life couldn't get any better. Kelly was living the life she didn't dare dream of but was somehow now a reality.

"Come outside with me," Logan said.

"Why? What's outside?"

"I want to make another one of your wishes come true."

"I don't believe I had any wishes left that you haven't granted."

"One more. Come on." She took Kelly's hand and led her out the back door to the large fenced-in yard.

"What is it?" Kelly asked. She turned a palm up. The light sprinkle had turned to a warm summer shower.

"This." Logan pulled her into her arms, gently swayed with her, and twirled her around. "We, my love, are dancing in the rain."

About the Author

Creativity for Joy Argento started young. She was only five, growing up in Syracuse, New York, when she picked up a pencil and began drawing animals. These days she calls Rochester home, and oil paints are her medium of choice. Her award-winning art has found its way into homes around the globe.

Writing came later in life for Joy. Her love of lesbian romance inspired her to try her hand at writing, and she found her first self-published novels well received. She is thrilled to be a part of the Bold Strokes family and has enjoyed their books for years.

Joy has three grown children who are making their own way in the world and six grandsons who are the light of her life.

Books Available from Bold Strokes Books

Curse of the Gorgon by Tanai Walker. Cass will do anything to ensure Elle's safety, but is she willing to embrace the curse of the Gorgon? (978-1-63679-395-5)

Dance with Me by Georgia Beers. Scottie Templeton mixes it up on and off the dance floor with sexy salsa instructor Marisa Reyes. But can Scottie get past Marisa's connection to her ex? (978-1-63679-359-7)

Gin and Bear It by Joy Argento. Opposites really can attract, and as Kelly and Logan work together to create a loving home for rescue cat Bear, they just might find one for themselves as well. (978-1-63679-351-1)

Harvest Dreams by Jacqueline Fein-Zachary. Planting the vineyard of their dreams, Kate Bauer and Sydney Barrett must resist their attraction while battling nature and their families, who oppose both the venture and their relationship. (978-1-63679-380-1)

Outside the Lines by Melissa Sky. If you had the chance to live forever, would you take it? Amara Rodriguez did and it sets her on a journey to find her missing mother and unravel the mystery of her own heart. (978-1-63679-403-7)

The No Kiss Contract by Nan Campbell. Workaholic Davy believes she can get the top spot at her firm if the senior partners think she's settling down and about to start a family, but she needs the delightful yet dubious Anna's help by pretending to be her fiancée. (978-1-63679-372-6)

The Value of Sylver and Gold by Michelle Larkin. When word gets out that former Boston homicide detective Reid Sylver can talk to the dead, the FBI solicits her help on a serial murder case, prompting Reid to assemble forces once again with Detective London Gold. (978-1-63679-093-0)

When It Feels Right by Tagan Shepard. Freshly out of the closet Marlene hasn't been lucky in love, but when it comes to her quirky new roommate Abby, everything just feels right. (978-1-63679-367-2)

Lucky in Lace by Melissa Brayden. Straitlaced stationery store owner Juliette Jennings's predictable life unravels when a sexy lingerie shop and its alluring owner move in next door. (978-1-63679-434-1)

Made for Her by Carsen Taite. Neal Walsh is a newly made member of the Mancuso crime family, but will her undeniable attraction to Anastasia Petrov, the wife of her boss's sworn enemy, be the ultimate test of her loyalty? (978-1-63679-265-1)

Off the Menu by Alaina Erdell. Reality TV sensation *Restaurant Redo* and its gorgeous host Erin Rasmussen will arrive to film in chef Taylor Mobley's kitchen. As the cameras roll, will they make the jump from enemies to lovers? (978-1-63679-295-8)

Pack of Her Own by Elena Abbott. When things heat up in a small town, steamy secrets are revealed between Alpha werewolf Wren Carne and her human mate, Natalie Donovan. (978-1-63679-370-2)

Return to McCall by Patricia Evans. Lily isn't looking for romance—not until she meets Alex, the gorgeous Cuban dance instructor at La Haven, a newly opened lesbian retreat. (978-1-63679-386-3)

So It Went Like This by C. Spencer. A candid and deeply personal exploration of fate, chosen family, and the vulnerability intrinsic in life's uncertainties. (978-1-63555-971-2)

Stolen Kiss by Spencer Greene. Anna and Louise share a stolen kiss, only to discover that Louise is dating Anna's brother. Surely, one kiss can't change everything…Can it? (978-1-63679-364-1)

The Fall Line by Kelly Wacker. When Jordan Burroughs arrives in the Deep South to paint a local endangered aquatic flower, she doesn't expect to become friends with a mischievous gin-drinking ghost who complicates her budding romance and leads her to an awful discovery and danger. (978-1-63679-205-7)

To Meet Again by Kadyan. When the stark reality of WW II separates cabaret singer Evelyn and Australian doctor Joan in Singapore, they must overcome all odds to find one another again. (978-1-63679-398-6)

Before She Was Mine by Emma L McGeown. When Dani and Lucy are thrust together to sort out their children's playground squabble, sparks fly leaving both of them willing to risk it all for each other. 978-1-63679-315-3)

Chasing Cypress by Ana Hartnett Reichardt. Maggie Hyde wants to find a partner to settle down with and help her run the family farm, but instead she ends up chasing Cypress. Olivia Cypress. 978-1-63679-323-8)

Dark Truths by Sandra Barret. When Jade's ex-girlfriend and vampire maker barges back into her life, can Jade satisfy her ex's demands, keep Beth safe, and keep everyone's secrets…secret? 978-1-63679-369-6)

Desires Unleashed by Renee Roman. Kell Murphy and Taylor Simpson didn't go looking for love, but as they explore their desires unleashed, their hearts lead them on an unexpected journey. 978-1-63679-327-6)

Maybe, Probably by Amanda Radley. Set against the backdrop of a viral pandemic, Gina and Eleanor are about to discover that loving another person is complicated when you're desperately searching for yourself. 978-1-63679-284-2)

The One by C.A. Popovich. Jody Acosta doesn't know what makes her more furious, that the wealthy Bergeron family refuses to be held accountable for her father's wrongful death, or that she can't ignore her knee-weakening attraction to Nicole Bergeron. 978-1-63679-318-4)

The Speed of Slow Changes by Sander Santiago. As Al and Lucas navigate the ups and downs of their polyamorous relationship, only one thing is certain: romance has never been so crowded. 978-1-63679-329-0)

Tides of Love by Kimberly Cooper Griffin. Falling in love is the last thing on either of their minds, but when Mikayla and Gem meet, sparks of possibility begin to shine, revealing a future neither expected. 978-1-63679-319-1)

Catch by Kris Bryant. Convincing the wife of the star quarterback to walk away from her family was never in offensive coordinator Sutton McCoy's game plan. But standing on the sidelines when a second chance at true love comes her way proves all but impossible. (978-1-63679-276-7)

Hearts in the Wind by MJ Williamz. Beth and Evelyn seem destined to remain mortal enemies but are about to discover that in matters of the heart, sometimes you must cast your fortunes to the wind. (978-1-63679-288-0)

Hero Complex by Jesse J. Thoma. Bronte, Athena, and their unlikely friends must work together to defeat Bronte's arch nemesis. The fate of love, humanity, and the world might depend on it. No pressure. (978-1-63679-280-4)

Hotel Fantasy by Piper Jordan. Molly Taylor has a fantasy in mind that only Lexi can fulfill. However, convincing her to participate could prove challenging. (978-1-63679-207-1)

Last New Beginning by Krystina Rivers. Can commercial broker Skye Kohl and contractor Bailey Kaczmarek overcome their pride and work together while the tension between them boils over into a love that could soothe both of their hearts? (978-1-63679-261-3)

Love and Lattes by Karis Walsh. Cat café owner Bonnie and wedding planner Taryn join forces to get rescue cats into forever homes—discovering their own forever along the way. (978-1-63679-290-3)

Repatriate by Jaime Maddox. Ally Hamilton's new job as a home health aide takes an unexpected twist when she discovers a fortune in stolen artwork and must repatriate the masterpieces and avoid the wrath of the violent man who stole them. (978-1-63679-303-0)

The Hues of Me and You by Morgan Lee Miller. Arlette Adair and Brooke Dawson almost fell in love in college. Years later, they unexpectedly run into each other and come face-to-face with their unresolved past. (978-1-63679-229-3)

A Haven for the Wanderer by Jenny Frame. When Griffin Harris comes to Rosebrook village, the love she finds with Bronte de Lacey creates a safe haven and she finally finds her place in the world. But will she run again when their love is tested? (978-1-63679-291-0)

A Spark in the Air by Dena Blake. Internet executive Crystal Tucker is sure Wi-Fi could really help small-town residents, even if it means putting an internet café out of business, but her instant attraction to the owner's daughter, Janie Elliott, makes moving ahead with her plans complicated. (978-1-63679-293-4)

Between Takes by CJ Birch. Simone Lavoie is convinced her new job as an intimacy coordinator will give her a fresh perspective. Instead, problems on set and her growing attraction to actress Evelyn Harper only add to her worries. (978-1-63679-309-2)

Camp Lost and Found by Georgia Beers. Nobody knows better than Cassidy and Frankie that life doesn't always give you what you want. But sometimes, if you're lucky, life gives you exactly what you need. (978-1-63679-263-7)

Felix Navidad by 'Nathan Burgoine. After the wedding of a good friend, instead of Felix's Hawaii Christmas treat to himself, ice rain strands him in Ontario with fellow wedding-guest— and handsome ex of said friend—Kevin in a small cabin for the holiday Felix definitely didn't plan on. (978-1-63679-411-2)

Fire, Water, and Rock by Alaina Erdell. As Jess and Clare reveal more about themselves, and their hot summer fling tips over into true love, they must confront their pasts before they can contemplate a future together. (978-1-63679-274-3)